"This is about that damned wedding again, isn't it?"

Marc strode toward her, until he was so close Melanie could smell his aftershave. "And you want me to believe that in three months you found someone who could replace what took us three years to build?" he continued. "Tell me something, Mel. Does he make you pant the way I did?"

The brush of his palm against her right nipple caused a massive shudder to travel the length of her body. She knew she should move away from him, protesting the familiar intimate touch, but she could only stand transfixed, wanting him to touch her...and more. "He makes me happy," Melanie said.

Marc frowned. "Outside of the bedroom. How's he going to make you feel inside?" He cupped her breast, very obviously avoiding contact with the straining tip.

She stifled a moan and tried to stop herself from leaning into his touch. "I don't think this...is a good idea, Marc. We should, um—" Melanie licked her lips, her gaze fixed on his mouth. "We should be discussing how we're going to catch the guy who's after me."

Marc slowly shook his head. "Sweetheart, the only thing I'm interested in catching right now is you."

As his mouth came down on hers, Melanie knew he already had.

Dear Reader,

Who can resist a sexy, rough-around-the-edges hero with a heart of gold? If you've read our first Temptation novel, *Constant Craving,* you know we can't. So we decided to try it again. And this time, not only is our hero, secret agent Marc McCoy, totally irresistible...he's got four dangerously attractive brothers cut from the same cloth. Is it any wonder we're calling them THE MAGNIFICENT McCOY MEN?

In *License to Thrill,* our intrepid hero, Marc McCoy is up against his ex-partner *and* former lover, Melanie Weber. Not only has she got another fiancé and a substantial secret that's bound to show up in say, seven months—she's also got a madman after her. But the story doesn't begin and end there. Oh, no.

We hope you enjoy Marc and Mel's adventurous journey to the altar. We'd love to hear what you think. Write to us at P.O. Box 12271, Toledo, OH 43612, or visit us at the web site we share with other Temptation authors at Temptationauthors.com. And be sure to watch for upcoming books featuring those oh-so-tempting McCoys....

Here's wishing you love, romance and happy endings.

Lori & Tony Karayianni

a.k.a. Tori Carrington

LICENSE TO THRILL
Tori Carrington

HARLEQUIN®

TORONTO • NEW YORK • LONDON
AMSTERDAM • PARIS • SYDNEY • HAMBURG
STOCKHOLM • ATHENS • TOKYO • MILAN • MADRID
PRAGUE • WARSAW • BUDAPEST • AUCKLAND

This one is for our remarkable editor, Brenda Chin, who
led us to the cliff's edge, then encouraged us to fly.
Thank you from the bottom of our hearts.

ISBN 0-373-25840-2

LICENSE TO THRILL

Copyright © 1999 by Lori and Tony Karayianni.

Printed in U.S.A.

1

JUST THINKING about Marc McCoy made Melanie Weber tingle with need. Even now. Especially now.

She slid her palms over the thick silk of the traditional wedding dress she was being fitted for. It was ironic, really. She had never thought of her relationship with Marc in the traditional sense. Still, she had expected they'd always be together. Always be partners. Always be lovers.

But that was three months ago. Before she realized Marc could never love her. Before she was injured in the line of duty. *Before she found out she was pregnant.*

Melanie reluctantly opened her eyes, then tugged her hands away from the wedding dress. A pinpoint of guilt started in her stomach and slowly spread through the rest of her body. The last person she should be thinking about was Marc McCoy. She'd carefully tucked him in the past the day Craig had generously offered to solve both their problems by proposing to her. She owed it to Craig to keep focused on their plans for the future. She owed it to herself to keep her thoughts away from the past and all that could never be.

Still she recognized the churning signs of panic that had been swirling in her since she and Craig had picked up their marriage license that morning. She'd felt the same way the day she had faced her mother to tell her that she wasn't majoring in business, as her mother so wanted. Only now she suspected hormones were more to blame for her anxiety—she hoped.

She turned slightly to view her profile. Funny, her jumbled thoughts didn't keep her from longing to wear a dress with an open décolletage neckline. But that was impossible. The fresh scar just below her left collarbone was difficult to look at, even for her. She could imagine what would happen if she flashed her gunshot wound to one hundred of Bedford, Maryland's, prominent citizens, much less her own mother. She shook her head. The seed-pearl-studded mock turtleneck that covered nearly every inch of her skin would have to do.

Melanie sucked in her stomach. If she didn't have the dress let out just a tad, she would split a seam in front of Craig Gaffney, God and everyone halfway down the aisle two days from now.

"Wouldn't *that* fuel Bedford's gossip hot line for at least a month?" she whispered to her reflection. As it was, she'd already given them enough to talk about. Scary, since they didn't even know the half of it.

"Joanie? Can you come here for a minute?" she called.

Her younger sister, Joanie, owned the Once Upon a Time Bridal Shoppe. It was just before closing, and with June looming but a few days away, Melanie's dress wasn't the only thing bursting at the seams. The shop was filled with stressed-out brides and overbearing mothers. She stuck her head into the hall. In the room opposite hers, Joanie slid a stray pin from the fabric peach forever around her wrist, then blew her hair from her eyes.

"Be with you in a minute, Melanie."

"Hey, be careful!" complained the bride whose dress Joanie skillfully worked on. "If you get so much as one drop of blood on this dress, I won't hesitate to sue."

Melanie ducked into her dressing room. Her sister could probably make a good chunk of change by videotaping some of the more interesting fittings and selling the footage to their grooms. But something like that would never occur to Joanie. Her sister's generous spirit and endless patience were the main reasons her business had grown so successful. They were also the reason she radiated happiness like a sweet perfume.

Melanie glimpsed her own rare smile in the mirror, then eyed the chair behind her. But no matter how much she wanted to rest her swollen feet, she didn't dare sit down. Not unless she decided to let out the dress herself in a way that would guarantee she couldn't wear it two days from now.

Saturday. Her wedding.

Her throat tightened, choking off her airway. She closed her eyes to ward off the unwanted reaction. Cold feet, that's all it was. A major case of cold feet. What more could it be?

"You can handle this, Mellie. I don't think I've met a braver woman than you. Aside from my Mary, of course."

The words conjured up the image of Sean's kind, time-marked face and sober green eyes.

Sean. Just Sean. She didn't know his last name. But his presence had been the only thing that had kept her sane during that long week in the hospital. Odd, she thought, because he had been little more than a stranger. A visitor, there for another patient, who had entered the wrong room and found her alone and crying. It was the only time she'd been left alone by her mother, Joanie and Craig, who had all meant well but hadn't a clue how to handle an injured secret service agent whose heart was breaking for the only person who hadn't visited.

Sean hadn't pried. He hadn't tried to comfort her. He'd simply handed her a tissue and sat next to her bed as if it had been her he had come to visit all along.

Picking up a bouquet sample, Melanie listlessly straightened a silk lily of the valley in the all-white waterfall bouquet. She hadn't seen Sean since she had been discharged, and hadn't expected to. But thinking about him made her realize how much she missed her father. Made her selfishly yearn to have him there if only for an hour or so. If only to walk her down the aisle.

Blinking back unexpected tears, she refocused on the bouquet. Merely looking at the fake flowers made her feel like a fake herself. She turned away, not sure she wanted to see the woman reflected in the smooth glass. Three months ago...

"Three months ago you were a fool in love with your career. And an even bigger fool in lust with Marc McCoy," she said softly.

She tossed the bouquet to the velvet chair and reached back to undo her dress, but she could barely move her arms. Joanie had trussed her in. It looked as if Joanie would have to let her out.

She sighed. "Just peachy."

Joanie poked her head around the corner. "Whatcha need?"

Melanie sighed with relief then tried to pinch the tiniest bit of fabric away from her waist. "You were right. It needs letting out."

"I was afraid of that." Joanie came to stand behind her, assessing the damage. "I really hate to tell you I told you so, but—"

"You told me so." Melanie watched her sister slide into her role as seamstress. While she may have spent the past eight years bucking tradition, Joanie had always been content with her life. More than that, she seemed to cherish the role she'd created for herself as everyone's best friend.

It struck Melanie as odd that she should be the one getting married when her sister was still inexplicably single.

Joanie sighed wistfully. "I really do love this dress." She smoothed the puckered seam. "I think it's the one I would pick, you know, if I was in your place." A shadow briefly moved over her pretty, freckled face. "You're lucky, you know? I don't think there's a time in my life when I can't remember Craig being around. And he's always had such a crush on you." She brushed a strand of red hair from her cheek. "You couldn't ask for a better man...."

Her soft words drifted off. Melanie watched her sister, wondering if she was going to mention that the most she and Craig had ever been were friends. The best of friends, but just friends. But her sister appeared to be thinking of something else entirely.

"Joanie?"

Her sister blinked then stared at Melanie in the mirror. "Sorry, must have drifted off there. I haven't had more than a couple hours sleep in the past two days."

Melanie looked at her a little more closely. "Are you sure that's all it is?"

"Sure? Of course I'm sure." She tried to pinch the back of the dress. "Wow, exactly how much weight have you put on since last month?"

She gently batted Joanie away from where she poked at her stomach. "Not all that much."

"Is it that time of the month?"

"No." Melanie wished it were that simple. If only she could tell Joanie why, exactly, she had grown out of her dress. But doing so would undermine Craig's generosity and would open up a whole different can of worms.

Two more days. Two more days and she could tell her sister and her mother.

Joanie pulled back. "No doubt about it. The seams need to be let out at least a half inch."

Melanie swallowed hard. The formal rehearsal dinner her mother had insisted on was only… She glanced at her watch. "Oh, God, I've only got a half hour to get to Bedford Inn."

Just then, an electronic bell rang, followed by a too-innocent, "Yoo-hoo!"

Joanie caught Melanie's gaze in the mirror.

"Mother," they said in unison.

"I'll take care of her," Melanie said, a heartbeat later. "You go finish up whatever you have to, so you can help me out at this dinner."

"Hmm. I don't know. A choice between dinner with Mother and your soon-to-be in-laws or playing voodoo doll with the bride next door? Tough call."

Melanie latched onto Joanie's arm. "Please don't make me go through this alone."

Her sister's green eyes widened in mild surprise. "Melanie, you're not facing a firing squad. Even if you were, you would be the one person I know who could handle it." She covered Melanie's hand with her own. "Okay, I'll be there." She laughed quietly. "But I have to say, you're on your own for the honeymoon."

Honeymoon. Melanie's stomach tightened to the point of pain.

She gathered fistfuls of her full skirt in her hands and led the way from the room. She'd like to say she was surprised by her mother's impromptu visit, but really couldn't. Her mother had always been good at reading her. She didn't doubt Wilhemenia Weber had picked up on the emotional turmoil she'd been going through for the past few months. And if she knew her mother, Wilhemenia wouldn't stop until she found out what was going on.

IN HIS JEEP outside the bridal shop, Marc McCoy absently rubbed the back of his neck, then flicked the air-conditioning on. He didn't know if it was the heat or his anxiety about what he was planning to do that made the temperature in the all-terrain vehicle intolerable, but if Mel took much longer, he was going to stalk in there after her. He grimaced. Who was he kidding? He wasn't going anywhere. He'd sit here and wait just as he had for the past forty-five minutes. All because he'd been too wrapped up in his thoughts when she'd gone in to see his plan through. Eight solid hours of planning, and he'd been knocked out of commission just at the thought of coming face-to-face with her for the first time in three months.

He directed the cool air vent toward his face, then let his gaze drift to the two glossy magazines on the passenger seat. He resisted the urge to grab the first one to find out exactly "what a woman looks for in a man." It wasn't long ago he wouldn't have been caught dead reading this stuff.

But Mel's absence in his life had left him with a gaping hole and long, endless nights that he tried to fill with reason.

He grabbed the magazines and shoved them under his seat.

He looked at his watch, then returned his attention to the shop.

He didn't know why, exactly, he had hesitated when he first spotted Melanie leaving her mother's house. For Pete's sake, he didn't even know why he hadn't marched right into the house the moment he got into town.

Frustrated with his hesitation, he shut off the car engine, then reached for the door handle. His hand froze on the sun-warmed metal. Melanie's mother was walking down the street looking like a woman on a mission.

"Uh-oh."

Instantly, he was reminded why he hadn't gone into the small house on Cherry Blossom Road. Because of Mel's mother.

What was she doing here? In order to do what he had to, Mel had to be alone. She'd gone into the shop alone, and he'd expected her to come out the same way. What he hadn't banked on was Wilhemenia Weber, who looked as though she'd come fresh from sucking on a dozen lemons, deciding to pay a visit.

She could be here to see Joanie, Marc thought. *I hope she's here to visit Joanie.*

Five minutes later, the late afternoon sun reflected off the bridal shop door, and he sat up straighter.

"Show time." Mel stepped onto the brick sidewalk. At least it looked like Mel. Grimacing, he slid down his sunglasses and squinted at the woman leaving. Yep, it was her all right. Minus the jeans, T-shirt and blue blazer she'd been wearing when she went in. Now she was decked out in one very short dress. But it was definitely her. *It's about time.* What did she do? Decide to wear her purchase home? He reached for the door handle again. If he lived to be two hundred, he'd never understand what it was with women and clothes. He still had at least eight pairs of Mel's shoes cluttering the closet in his town house. Keeping his gaze focused on Mel, he began to climb out...then froze.

There weren't very many things Marc McCoy, Secret Service Agent, third of five proudly macho male siblings, was afraid of. But he was man enough to admit that Wilhemenia Weber was one of them. And when she followed Mel out of the shop, she threw a wrench the size of a semi truck into his plans.

"Damn."

Marc fought the urge to sink down in his seat. Not only to keep Mel from spotting him, but to prevent her mother from focusing her fault-finding gaze on him. Oh, yeah, he'd met her once. And that one time was enough to know the woman would never like him. He grimaced, finding it difficult to believe it was just over three months ago, before that stupid discussion about love and before Mel's injury, that she'd talked him into going home for Sunday dinner.

Mrs. Weber's disapproving stare had started when he sat on the couch, causing the thick plastic furniture cover to crackle in a way that had made him flinch even as Mel laughed. The Stare had followed him throughout dinner, where Wilhemenia had jerked his soup bowl out from under his nose—apparently because he wasn't convincing enough while trying to choke back the thick, cold green stuff—and ending when she'd practically slammed the door on him when he'd only been halfway out.

The only saving grace was that Mel had taken a perverse sort of pleasure in the whole ordeal. But he absolutely drew the line at returning to that woman's home. Unless she took that stupid plastic off her furniture and ordered in for pizza and beer.

He sobered, realizing that would never happen. Not until Mel invited him back into her life.

His gaze followed mother and daughter down the sidewalk of the quaint little town of Bedford. What was more than a little unsettling was that he still wished Mrs. Weber had liked him…at least a little.

The risk of being spotted gone, Marc scanned the street before he slowly switched his attention to Mel. And found it suddenly difficult to breathe.

He couldn't quite put his finger on it, but she looked different somehow. Her blond hair was slightly longer, brushing the top of her shoulders in a curly way that caught the rays of the early evening sun. But that wasn't it. Then it dawned on him. It was the dress. Well, not the dress, exactly, but the fact that she was wearing it. In muted pink with shiny flowery things stamped on the fabric, it was exactly the type of thing Mel wouldn't have been caught dead in before. He appreciated the sway of her bottom, thinking he'd have been okay with her wearing feminine attire if she'd asked him. But she hadn't. In fact, aside from the brief meeting when they'd first been assigned to work together, he'd never seen her in a dress. And then she'd been wearing a knee-length black skirt. This thing…this thing barely brushed the middle of her thighs.

Then there were those heels.

Growing more than a little hot and bothered, Marc tugged at the neck of his T-shirt. The shoes added a good three inches to her five feet seven inches. That would bring the top of her head to his nose rather than his chin when they came face-to-face.

Mrs. Weber turned her head in his direction. Marc slumped in his seat, jamming his knees against the dashboard in the process. He cursed. But the words barely exited his mouth when Mel nearly toppled right off those high, sexy heels. He grinned, forgetting the pain shooting up his knees for a second. Now *that* was more like the Mel he knew and—

He bit back the word, an audible gulp filling the interior of the Jeep. What did he know about love? Hadn't Mel told him during their first and only argument that he didn't know diddly about love?

No, he didn't, couldn't love her. He just liked Mel's sexy backside enough to think it worth protecting from the guy who'd already shot her once.

"Oh, yeah? Then tell me something, McCoy. Why is that damn engagement ring you've been carrying around for three months burning a hole in your pocket?"

ADVENTURE, FREEDOM and hot sex are overrated. Melanie squeezed her eyes shut and repeated the sentence slowly.

"Melanie, dear, there are guests present."

She cracked her eyelids open to take in a generous view of Wilhemenia, who sat across from her in the dining area of the Bedford Inn. She wasn't sure why, but lately everything her mother said, no matter how innocuous, got under her skin. She offered a patient smile. "Of course there are guests present. It's my rehearsal dinner. I invited them, remember?"

She took in the gilded antique chairs, the crisp white damask tablecloths and the pretty flowered wallpaper, wondering exactly why the traditional event was called a rehearsal. It wasn't as though she or Craig needed pointers on how to walk down the aisle. That was a no-brainer. She smiled at Craig's father, who sat adjacent to her, and suppressed the urge to fidget, sure the unladylike move would elicit another public reprimand from her mother. Then realization settled in. The rehearsal part of it didn't have so much to do with her and Craig. Rather it was a preview of what holidays would look like from here on out.

The tickle of panic that had been with her all day grew to a pang.

Melanie tried to shake the images that crowded her mind. But like an unwelcome visit from the ghost of Christmas future, she envisioned her mother perched on the edge of a couch making comments that always somehow seemed like criticisms about the Christmas tree and covertly trying to get at the nonexistent dust bunnies under the coffee table with her ever-present embroidered handkerchief.

And Craig's parents? Melanie watched them as she chewed a bite of cold roast beef. Okay, so his father was a bit…overbearing. Suspicious almost. Which was only fair given the suddenness of the upcoming nuptials. Melanie's cheeks heated. Craig's mother, on the other hand, was almost effusively nice. Likely a result of spending the past forty years trying to compensate for her husband's bad manners. And her desire for grandchildren from her only child. The roast beef stuck in Melanie's throat. Doris was going to get one of those sooner than she expected.

Guilt ballooned to challenge the panic.

Craig's mother smiled at her brightly. Melanie smiled back, the tongs of her fork screeching against china.

She purposely avoided looking at Wilhemenia.

"Scary, isn't it?"

"Hmm?" She glanced at Craig, who sat next to her.

He leaned a little closer and lowered his voice so only she could hear. "The thought of these guys being in the same room for more than five minutes at a stretch." He cleared his throat. "Just getting my own parents to spend that much time together is asking for trouble."

His familiar grin eased her discomfort as he unwittingly fit his own welcome image in with the others stamped in her mind. It didn't surprise her that he'd been thinking the same thing she had. Throughout their nearly lifelong friendship, Craig and she had always understood each other.

She watched as the grin vanished from his face. He tugged at his tie. She thought he must be feeling as awkward as she was. He leaned in her direction again. "When this infernal thing is over, we need to talk."

"Sure, we can do that." Melanie was almost relieved to focus on someone else. She had been so wrapped up in her own thoughts, she hadn't considered that Craig might be as nervous about all this as she was. But the fact that his request was so very serious scared her. Was he having second thoughts?

She glanced up to find the table had gone suspiciously silent. "How about this heat wave?" she said, not comfortable with the way her mother was watching her.

Doris made some comparison between the heat and a tin roof that Melanie missed, but Craig's burst of laughter made her sigh.

Why can't you be more like Marc?

She jerked involuntarily at the unwelcome thought, sending her fork sailing through the air. She watched in horror as it spiraled above the table, prongs over stem, prongs over stem.... Finally it landed neatly in the middle of her mother's plate, spearing her roasted potatoes.

"Melanie!"

Her cheeks felt on fire. Of all the places for the sucker to land. She tightly clasped her hands in her lap where they were unlikely to do more damage.

"Pardon me."

"Are you all right?" Craig asked.

Melanie made a show of watching her mother pluck the foreign piece of silver from her food.

Look at him, she ordered herself. She did.

It wasn't that Craig Gaffney wasn't attractive. He was appealing in an all-American way that included surfer good looks, wide grin and a sharp mind for drugs. Pharmaceuticals, she amended. She thanked the waiter when he brought her another set of linen-wrapped silverware. Her mother cleared her throat. Melanie carefully freed the silver from the white linen and picked up the clean fork, though she didn't think she could swallow another bite of food.

Craig had a great sense of humor. Did it really matter that he sometimes didn't grasp a punch line? Or that his capacity for humor had somewhat dwindled since they announced their engagement?

She picked up her wineglass and took a hefty sip only to

realize she shouldn't be drinking. She forced herself to swallow, then coughed. Craig's father narrowed his eyes, watching her far too closely.

"Wrong pipe," she said quietly.

Her fiancé was also very comfortable to be around, she continued, reviewing her Pro-Marriage to Craig column. A quality that had instantly cemented their friendship nearly twenty-five years ago when they were in kindergarten. He didn't judge her the way most people did then…and now. She glanced in her mother's direction. Wilhemenia was frowning…again. No, Craig had always accepted her for who she was. Which made accepting his proposal all too easy when she'd spilled her troubles to him.

Craig leaned toward her, giving her a hefty whiff of his cologne. *I can change that.* He lowered his voice. "You don't feel like you, well, you know, have to—"

"Throw up?" she said a little too loudly.

He didn't laugh. Instantly, she realized why. No one else at the table knew she was pregnant.

She searched for a way to cover her mistake. "I think I'm suffering from a case of pre-wedding nerves. Otherwise, I'm fine. Really." Which was true enough. She hadn't suffered through a moment of morning sickness, and she was two weeks into her second trimester.

Pregnancy. Baby. Marriage.

Suddenly, Melanie did feel sick.

Sick with fear.

What did she know about being a mother?

"I never thought Melanie would be the first of my girls to marry," Wilhemenia was saying to Doris. The comment caused Craig's father's gaze to sharpen. "Joanie was always the better bet."

More wife material, Melanie silently added, wondering exactly where her sister was and why she wasn't here defending her. And why was her mother discussing her as though she weren't even at the table?

Craig's mother tittered. "But you have to agree, she'll make a handsome bride."

Archie drained half his glass of beer. "Tell me again why you two are in such a rapid-fire hurry to have Pastor Pitts marry you?"

Melanie started. Craig squeezed her hand and said, "I think a twenty-five-year courtship is long enough, don't you, Pumpkin?"

Pumpkin? Okay, so soon she'd look as though she'd swallowed a pumpkin, but still... "You did ask me to marry you on the playground, didn't you, Pookems?"

He blinked at her.

Melanie was aghast at her behavior. She resisted propping her elbows on the table and covering her face as she considered exactly what was going to hit her and Craig once everyone found out she was pregnant. And learned just how far along she was. It wouldn't take a Ph.D. to figure out the math. Craig had been not only out of town at the time of conception—he'd been out of the country. In New Guinea. Doing whatever pharmacists did in third-world countries. That wasn't fair, because she knew exactly what he had been doing. While she...

Melanie finally gave in and rested her forehead against her hand, ignoring her mother's stare.

God, she *was* going to be sick.

She pushed away from the table. Everyone grabbed their glasses and silverware to keep them from becoming deadly projectiles. Tears burned her eyes. Could she possibly make this dinner any worse?

"Excuse me. I'm going to..." *What? Lock myself in a bathroom stall until the world makes sense?* "Powder my nose."

Her mother neatly placed her napkin next to her plate. "I'll come with you."

"No!"

The occupants of the head table stared at her in stunned silence, as did the half of the population of Bedford that had been invited to the dinner. Melanie tried to control her voice. "I mean, thank you, Mother, but I can see to this my-self." Her mother appeared ready to argue. "I'm fine. *Really.*"

Melanie shakily stood her ground. Surprisingly, it worked. Her mother sat down. "Very well, dear."

Melanie looked for the tiny bag she'd brought with her, then saw it lying on the floor. She stopped herself from crawling under the table for it, smiled at everyone, then stepped as casually as she could toward the hallway.

She felt awful. Her stomach was upset, she felt bloated and her swollen feet ached. But it was more than that. She felt out of her element. Usually in command of every situation, she now felt inexplicably vulnerable. As soon as she was in the hall, she collapsed against the wall, blinking back hot tears. What was the matter with her? Hormones? Or did some part of her realize she was making the biggest mistake of her life?

Out of eyeshot of everyone in the dining room, she slowly slid her hands down her stomach, resting them over the exact spot where even now her child was growing within her.

Marc's child.

She briefly closed her eyes, wondering again if not telling Marc about her condition was such a good idea.

She wiped the dampness from her cheeks. Too late now, wasn't it?

Besides, Marc had made it clear he wasn't interested in anything permanent. She reached down and slid her aching feet from the torturous contraptions Joanie called shoes and tried to work the heel off one. She couldn't very well wear them if they were broken, could she? It wouldn't budge. She started in the direction of the rest rooms before someone caught her trying to snap the heel off from the other one.

Inside the pink-and-gold rest room, she locked herself into a stall and sank down on the seat. She needed a few moments to herself. Bolstering minutes to take a deep breath and pull herself together. She had to. Not for her sake. For her baby's. And, a guilty part reminded her, for Craig. He deserved better than a cranky bride who abandoned him to his mother-in-law.

Melanie swallowed hard, appreciating if not particularly overjoyed with the humor of the situation. After using up the better part of her life trying not to upset the delicate balance of her relationship with her mother, she'd spent the past eight years going through an odd, ambitious sort of rebellion. Not a planned one, by any means. But during her first year at college, all the emotion—all the hunger for adventure she had secretly craved—had just kind of gushed out, overwhelming her with its intensity. She'd been as unable to deny the change in herself as she would have been able to keep the sun from warming her skin.

Then, three months ago, she had paid for that "coming out" of sorts. But tucking away the thrill-seeking Melanie Weber was not an easy task.

The outer door opened. "Yoo-hoo."

Melanie closed her eyes and clutched her shoes, half wishing she could climb on top of the toilet so her mother couldn't see her stocking feet from under the door. Not that it mattered. She peeked through her eyelids to find her mother angling her head to peer through the thin crack between the hinges.

"I'm in here, Mother."

"Oh!"

She had to give her mother credit. At least she attempted to act as though she hadn't just been gaping into a closed stall.

She heard the door next to hers close. There was no rustling of clothes, meaning her mother wasn't doing anything in her stall, either.

"Mother?"

"Yes, Melanie?"

"Why are you so afraid I won't go through with…well, you know, with marrying Craig?"

There was silence, then the distinct sound of the toilet paper roll going around in circles. Melanie gave in to a sudden smile. At least her mother was attempting to make the situation look somehow normal.

"Well…I have to admit, I am a little concerned about your unusual behavior these past couple days." Wilhemenia paused. "I don't know, your behavior reminds me so much of that time you came home from university for the summer and neglected to tell me you'd changed your major from business to pre-law." She made a quiet sound. "I won't say a word about how your choice of careers after graduation disappointed me."

You don't have to say anything because you already have. Every time you want me to do something I'm against.

Melanie propped her shoes on a metal shelf then toyed with her own toilet paper. "And do you really think hovering over me like a—" *jailer?* "—like a mother hen is going to prevent that from happening?"

Another brief silence. "It's not like that at all. I…I just want to be here if you need anyone to talk to."

Melanie caught herself ripping the paper to shreds, the pieces floating to land around her feet.

"Melanie?"

God, she was crying again. If she kept up the waterworks, she'd end up floating down the aisle on a wave of her own tears.

Her mother spoke again. "*Is* there anything you want to talk about?"

Melanie opened her mouth, but nothing came out. She swiped at her damp cheeks.

Her mother cleared her throat. "If this is about that Marc character, you should just put him out of your mind right now."

Melanie released a long, silent sigh, the words a vivid reminder of exactly why she couldn't talk to her mother.

"He's not the marrying kind, you know. More little boy than man. You'd only be miserable."

Melanie nodded, hating her mother's words but agreeing with them nonetheless. She was beginning to suspect that the only thing worse than being *without* Marc McCoy was being *with* him.

"Mom?" The shortening of the word mother should have sounded foreign, but oddly enough it didn't. "Did you love Dad?"

For the life of her, she couldn't figure out why she had asked that. Her father had died when she was three, right after Joanie was born. What did ancient history—especially her mother's ancient history—have to do with what was happening now?

"Never mind. Forget I just asked that question." Melanie got up and collected her shoes.

"Melanie?"

She stopped midway toward the door. "Yes?"

"I..." Wilhemenia's voice trailed off. "I just wanted to tell you that all I've ever wanted is for you to be happy."

Some of Melanie's tension melted away. "Marrying Craig will make me happy, Mom. Thanks." She gestured vaguely, though her mother couldn't see her. "Thanks for putting everything back into perspective."

Clutching her shoes in one hand, she opened the outer door. She skidded to a dead stop, finding herself nose-to-chin with a whole different barrier.

Marc McCoy.

Melanie's breath gusted from her.

That can't be right. This was her rehearsal dinner. Marc shouldn't be anywhere near the inn or the rest rooms, much less her, right now. Yet there he was, big as life and twice as tantalizing. She stumbled backward.

"Wrong way. You want to come out." Marc folded his fingers around her wrist and tugged her the rest of the way into the hall. Melanie's knees felt about as substantial as baby food. She had no choice but to lean into him, causing a wave of longing to flow through her body. Suddenly, three months seemed like a very short period of time, indeed.

"What's going—"

"Shh." Marc laid a finger against her mouth. The simple action was maddeningly sensual. Her gaze was glued to his lips. But rather than kissing her, he set her purposefully away from him, confounding her even more. She moved her hand to the side of her throat, feeling her pulse thrumming wildly, her skin searingly hot.

"Interesting conversation you and your mother were having in there," he said.

Melanie avoided his gaze. "You heard?"

She didn't realize what he was doing until he slid a mop handle through the door handle, securely barring her mother inside the ladies' room.

A hysterical laugh tickled Melanie's throat. She couldn't count the times she would have loved to lock her mother in a room. But wishful thinking was one thing; willful doing was quite another. She battled the irresponsible emotion.

"Let's go," Marc said, taking her hand.

Let's go? Had he actually just said, "Let's go"?

Melanie dug in her heels as best she could, considering she wore no shoes. Her stocking feet slid across the tile as Marc hauled her toward the parking lot. She swatted at him with the lethal shoes in her free hand.

"Hold on a minute, McCoy. Just where do you think you're taking me?"

He stopped. "Why, out of here, of course."

Melanie stared at the man who had the power to overturn every one of her well-laid plans. Her stomach pitched as she realized he intended to do just that.

Then he had the nerve to grin. Grin! Okay, he was rubbing the spot where her spike heel had nicely connected, but otherwise there was no evidence she had done anything more than blow a strand of his rich brown hair out of place.

"Hello, Mel. Miss me?"

Miss him? About as much as a bad sunburn. But her heart started to murmur something else. Melanie ignored it.

"What are you doing here? You weren't on the guest list. I know because I drew it up."

"I penciled myself in." Marc's reflective sunglasses prevented her from seeing his brown eyes, but his smile told her more than she wanted to know. His head tilted forward as he took a languid look over the tight-fitting silk of her dress, then up to where the sleek material hugged her waist and breasts. "Put on some weight, haven't you, Mel?"

Scorching heat spilled over her cheeks again as she fought the desire to cover her stomach. *He doesn't know,* she reminded herself.

"Looks good on you."

While her physical dimensions had altered a bit since she last saw Marc, he hadn't changed a bit. At six foot two, he was two hundred pounds of raw, muscled male. His military background was evident only in his tall posture. The easygoing grin and lazy casualness were pure Marc, as were his black T-shirt, jeans and the suede vest she knew concealed the 9mm revolver he always carried.

The mop handle rattled against the door. "Melanie?"

Oh, God. Mother. "You know, it's not very nice to go around locking people in bathrooms." Melanie tugged her hand, but he only tightened his hold. "Marc!"

"What?"

"Let me go." She considered whacking him with her shoe again. He finally released her.

"Aw, now is that any way to treat an old boyfriend?"

A handsome grimace creased Marc's face. A face she had tried to forget. A face chock-full of remarkable features she sometimes found herself wishing her child would inherit. *Their child.* Melanie swallowed hard.

"Ex-partner, then," he said quietly. "Surely you have a few minutes for your ex-partner."

Partners. Yes, they had been at least that. Although not in any permanent sense of the word, despite her present condition. Their partnership had been more professional than personal, and she had been dumb to forget that even for a second. As special agents for the Treasury Department's Secret Service Division, they had worked together for two years. Up until Melanie decided it was time to get out.

Wrong choice of words. She hadn't decided anything. The decision had been made for her. By a fellow agent who had turned his gun on her...and by a doctor's innocent words.

"Ex-partners do not lie in wait when all they want to do is catch up," she said softly. "What do you want?"

Marc had always been good at his job. When he wanted, he could be formidable. His physical appearance alone was enough to scare off any number of fanatics hoping for a shot at stardom by targeting a political candidate. But in his downtime, Melanie knew him to be an irresistibly handsome, rambunctious little boy who usually took nothing and no one seriously. Which gave her a definite advantage over him.

Melanie bit her lip. She didn't want to think like an agent anymore. In fact, she hadn't thought about her previous career for at least—well, half a day. Hooker had called her from jail that morning, after a two-month silence, despite court orders for him not to do so. Hearing his voice before she broke the connection had rattled her as much as his previous calls, not to mention the countless letters he'd sent her, which she had returned unopened. Out of the need to feel safe, she'd strapped her firearm on. An irrational act, considering Hooker was in custody.

"Yoo-hoo. Melanie, there's something blocking the door. Could you open it, please?" There were rattling sounds as her mother tried to open it herself. "Melanie?"

Melanie swallowed hard, feeling Marc's gaze hone in on her despite the sunglasses. She suppressed a shiver.

"You're going to have to call off the wedding, Mel."

She blinked. "What?" she whispered.

"You heard me. Tell the poor guy you agreed to marry you're sorry, but there's been a change in plans."

Hysterical laughter again threatened to erupt from Melanie's throat. She thought of all the plans that had been made, the guests who had been invited, and realized she'd drop everything in a heartbeat if she thought for a minute that Marc loved her. But he'd already made it clear he didn't and never would.

No, Marc's appearance was just one more unfair occurrence in a day chock-full of them.

"Not on your life." She surveyed him. She noticed the way he stood, all too handsome and deceptively relaxed, then watched the casual way he shifted his weight toward the bathroom door. Melanie's gaze slid to the barrier, and her heart gave a triple beat.

"Melanie? Who's out there with you? Is it Craig? Maybe he can help—"

Melanie dove for the mop handle. Before she could pull it free, Marc's arms snaked around her waist. She gasped and thrust her elbow into his stomach with all the force she could muster, given her restricting apparel. She met with what felt like reinforced steel. While she'd gone a little soft around the middle, he'd gotten more than a bit harder.

"Come on, Mel, don't make me go to Plan B," he murmured.

Plan B? What was he talking about? And why did dread and anticipation spread through her at the humor in his voice? She stilled. "You can let go of me now," she said with forced calm.

"Why? So you can try to let your mother out again? No way. I've been trying to get you alone all afternoon. Now that I've got you, I intend to do what I came for." His breath stirred the hair over her right ear. She was powerless to stop an obvious shiver. "You *are* happy to see me."

She tried to loosen his grasp, but again he tightened it.

"Come on, Marc, where am I going to go?" She wriggled against him, hating that he could read her reaction so well.

"Mmm."

Melanie's knees threatened to give out at the sound of his soft hum. His palms had flattened against her hips and now nudged up toward the underside of her breasts. She gasped, every traitorous part of her body craving that all too familiar touch.

Marc buried his face in her hair and breathed deeply. "God, I forgot what it was like to touch you."

Need grew within her again, stronger this time. "Please let me go." She hated the helpless quality of her voice and tried to insert some metal. "Or else I'll do something you won't find very pleasant."

His chuckle stirred more than her hair. "You always were one for idle threats, weren't you?"

Somehow she found the energy to do what she had to. Curling her fingers around one of the shoes, she swung it backward, heel first, hitting her intended target. Air rushed from Marc's body. He stumbled back, releasing his hold on her and reaching for his crotch.

"How idle was that?" Melanie whispered. Clutching her shoes in one hand, she reached for the mop handle with her other.

"Oh, no, you don't," Marc said.

Melanie's stomach gave a small flip as she struggled to open the bathroom door. She nearly had the mop free when Marc drove it home.

"Why did I think this would be easy?" he murmured.

The world tilted beneath Melanie. By the time everything stopped spinning, she found herself draped over one of Marc's wide shoulders, her shoes bouncing off the tiled floor. Her eyes were parallel with his jeans-clad rear end. And oh, what a rear end it was, too. Too bad she wasn't in the mood to enjoy it at the moment.

What was she thinking? She didn't want to enjoy anything about Marc. Not now. Not ever again. In two days she was getting married. And not to Marc. Because Marc had a bad habit of disappearing when she needed him most.

"I can't believe you just did that!"

"Yeah, well, believe it," he murmured. "I don't care what they say, sometimes drastic measures are necessary."

They? Who were they? God, she wished some of this mad situation would start making sense.

Marc suddenly stilled. "Everything's fine, sir. You just go on about your business."

Melanie peeked around his hips to see her uncle Fred worrying his tie in his hands. Bedford's most prominent banker scurried toward the men's room across the hall, not even attempting to help. Melanie suddenly wanted to cry.

A tentative knocking sounded on the ladies' room door. "Melanie? Are you all right?"

Drawing in a fortifying breath, she said, "I'm fine, Mother." Aside from feeling like a sack of flour. "Feel better now?" she asked him quietly.

"Much, thank you," Marc said lightly. "Now, tell me how I go about making you see reason."

"Reason? I'm not the one who just threw someone over her shoulder."

She felt a hot hand on her ankle. She fidgeted and tried to see what he was doing.

"Hold still, or you'll find a hand right where I'm sure you least want it," he said. "Tell me, Mel, do you still take that neat little nickel-plated .25 everywhere you go?"

Melanie's eyes widened as he cupped her right heel, then slowly slid his fingers up her calf, tickling the back of her knee. "Marc! Get your hands off me, you overgrown—"

His probing ceased just short of her panties. He stood silently for long moments. Melanie didn't dare breathe. Awareness tingled everywhere his hand had touched, and even now neglected parts of herself pleaded for the pleasure they knew Marc could bring.

"Satisfied?" she croaked.

"Not nearly," Marc said quietly. He moved his hand across her backside, eliciting a gasp, then slowly began down her other leg. "There she blows," he said, pulling her .25 free from her thigh holster.

Melanie groaned and pushed against him in exasperation.

"Tell me, Mel, does your fiancé know what you hide under your skirt?" he asked, not removing his hand. Instead, he caressed the spot around her empty holster with feathery, fiery flicks of his callused thumb. She wriggled against him, threatening to topple herself to the floor. The way she figured it, anything was better than subjecting herself to Marc's all-knowing touch.

"Put me down."

His hand abruptly disappeared from her leg.

Rather than relief, Melanie felt nothing but disappointment. She held on for dear life as he bent to pick up her shoes.

"I will," he said, the lazy teasing back in his voice. "Eventually."

2

MARC TOOK IN everything and everyone in the parking lot in one glance. He hadn't expected to spot Tom Hooker lurking in the shadows—the shooter who could even now have his gunsights set on Mel—but he hadn't expected Hooker to escape custody the day before, either. No matter how overloaded his senses were with Mel's nearness, he couldn't forget that all evidence indicated Hooker was not only on a direct route to Mel, he was armed to the teeth, as well.

He picked up his pace.

Well, *that* hadn't exactly gone as planned, had it? He shifted Mel's weight more evenly over his shoulder, ignoring her attempts to get him to let her down. Ignoring, too, the warmth of having her body against his again, even given present circumstances. He strode toward his Jeep, parked in the far corner of the lot. The smell of new fabric mingled with Mel's soft, subtle perfume. Linden flowers. That's what he had always likened the scent to. She had always insisted it was jasmine. One of these days he'd take her to his family home in Manchester, Virginia, to show her the linden tree in the back yard. The tree's brief but fragrant blossoms were the closest he'd ever gotten to any type of flower in the all-male household in which he'd been raised. Of course, while Mel shared his small town background, the only flowers likely to be found in her yard were of the rose variety.

"Where are you taking me?" Mel asked, wiggling to free herself from his hold.

"Cut it out, Mel. You're just making this harder." He

tried not to focus on the way her breasts jiggled against his back and gave her bottom another squeeze. He grinned at her gasp.

"Is that what this is all about?" Her voice was raspy. Her movements stopped. "Are you doing this to cop one last feel?"

"Feel?" He opened the back door of the Jeep, thinking that touching her again would indeed be reason enough for him to kidnap her. "No, Mel." He laid her across the back seat, causing the tight, short skirt to shimmy up her thighs, baring her legs and other more secret areas for his scrutiny. He tossed her shoes into the back, his gaze glued to the tiny scrap of material that masqueraded as underwear. It didn't come close to disguising the soft, down-covered swell of sweet flesh it covered.

He concentrated on the tightening of his throat instead of the swelling in another area of his anatomy. Oh, how he longed to claim that mouth of hers with his, to skim his hands down her lush body, to trail a finger along the border of those panties, slowly, teasingly, watching as the silky material dampened with her reaction....

He reined in his thoughts. Speaking of groins, he'd be better off protecting his whenever he was on this side of her feet. The thought hit him just as she thrust her foot toward him.

He caught her ankle. Despite her actions, in her face he read the same longing he felt. He hadn't realized how much he missed small moments like these. When everything but Mel vanished into the background. When just knowing how quickly he could make her come apart sent his blood pounding through his veins and opened a peculiar sort of weightlessness in his stomach.

He shifted his hand up her calf, the languid move hiding the way he shook inside.

"Marrying Craig will make me happy."

Melanie's words to her mother just moments earlier echoed through his mind. His hand froze as he slowly tore his gaze from her face. The feel of her warm, satiny skin beneath his palm made him fear it would take a crowbar to lift his hand.

A glance around the parking area reminded him where he was and what he was doing. Gradually, the sound of his heartbeat lessened, and the drone of cars passing on the nearby street increased. He finally moved his hand and swallowed...hard.

"Nice view," he said, keeping his voice carefully neutral.

When he dared look at her again, her cheeks were flushed with color and she was avoiding his gaze. But it was the rough sound of her voice that betrayed her most of all. "Yeah, well, you might want to get a good look while you can." Mel battled with the skirt, pulling on the hem until it somewhat covered her.

I don't need to look. Everything about you is already burned into my memory.

Marc forced himself to reach for the handcuffs he'd left on the floor. He leaned toward her, careful not to let things spiral out of control again. Afraid it wouldn't take much.

"I'm really sorry about doing this, Mel." He grasped her wrist. He expected a struggle, but surprisingly he encountered little. He grimaced as he tugged her arm over her head. The metal teeth of the cuffs caught as he attached one side to her wrist, threaded the other through the handgrip above the window, then dragged her other arm up. He tried not to notice the way her chest heaved with every breath as he caught her legs under his weight. He took his sunglasses off and tossed them to the front seat. He was about to pull away when his gaze snagged on hers again.

God, it had been a long time. Too long.

Marc stretched his neck, thinking an ordinary man would be a goner with one look into Mel's face right now. She looked altogether too kissable, too damned sexy.

Luckily he'd never considered himself an ordinary man. He came from four generations of McCoys who had served in the military or law enforcement or both. He had once been a Marine. Nope, none of the five current McCoy brothers, if asked, would ever admit to knowing the meaning of the word *ordinary*.

Only problem was, the pep talk wasn't doing diddly to douse his need to taste her lips....

Before he knew it, he was leaning closer to her, his breath mingling with her wine-scented breath. He eyed her mouth, groaning at the way she moistened her lips with a quick dart of her pink tongue.

"Marc, you better, um, not do what I think you're about to."

"Do what?" *Get it under control, McCoy.* "Kiss you?"

She made a sound that was somewhere between a whimper and a warning. It took Herculean strength to leave her mouth untouched, her lips slightly parted, no matter how much he wanted to claim both. *Because* of how much he wanted to. Instead he brushed his lips against the sensitive shell of her ear. "Remember when we used the handcuffs for reasons that were...not professionally correct?"

"That...that was a long time ago." She fairly croaked.

"Not so long ago that you can't remember." Not so long ago that he couldn't remember, either. Even now he hardened painfully at the images that slipped through his mind. Sex with Mel had always been intense. But, somehow, looking at her now, he found it hard to believe this prissily dressed example of upper-middle-class bliss could still be an inventive spitfire between the sheets.

He heard the click of her swallow as she moved restlessly beneath him.

Oh, she remembered, all right. He could tell by the way she arched against him even as she sought to put more distance between them. Impossible, given their current position.

"I don't think it's a good idea for either of us to remember," she said quietly, turning her head away when he would have pressed his mouth against her jawline.

He forced himself to pull back. "I think it's the best idea I've heard in a long time."

She turned her head toward him. "Just one of the many examples of how differently we think, isn't it?"

He recognized the shadow of pain in her eyes. He'd seen it once before. The night before she was shot. The night they'd had their first and, as luck would have it, last argument. The night she had asked if he loved her.

Remembering the moment, Marc found swallowing almost impossible. But upon closer examination, he discovered there was something else in the depths of her eyes that was somehow unlike the pain she had so clearly felt then.

Before he could pinpoint exactly what, she moved one of her legs up, catching him off guard, though her stockings guaranteed her attempts were ineffective. He grimaced, thinking it was a good thing he'd tossed her shoes into the back or he'd have been in trouble.

"You're getting rusty, Mel." He patted her legs then reluctantly drew back. "I guess a dress and a couple months under Mother Wilhemenia's roof will do that to a person."

He watched the color return to her cheeks, though she still refused to meet his gaze. "And you're still as reckless as you always were, aren't you, Marc?"

"You used to tell me my...how did you put it? My adventurous nature was what you loved about me." He cringed at the loose use of the L-word.

"What?" The cuffs clanked as she shifted to look at him. "I never said I loved that about you. That trait is exactly what made me—what made us so different."

Marc eased himself out of the car and closed the door. He drew in a deep breath and worked his shoulders to loosen the muscles there. Yes, Mel had always appealed to him in a way he'd never wanted to examine too closely, but this… He thrust his hand through his hair, frustrated by his inability to define what he was feeling. One thing he did know was that he'd have to control it if he was going to protect Mel in the way she needed to be protected. And if he was going to get her back into his life.

He glanced toward the inn. Why didn't it surprise him to find Mrs. Weber marching through the door? He grimaced, watching as she motioned to a man about his own age. Marc clutched the driver's door handle. Mel's groom, he guessed.

No, this wasn't going as planned at all.

Then again, nothing with Mel had ever really gone as planned. If it had, she would still be with him and the division and she wouldn't be getting ready to marry some other fool on Saturday morning, putting herself at more risk than she knew. And making him feel lonelier than he'd ever thought possible.

He climbed in and slammed the door so hard the Jeep rocked. He started the engine.

"Where are you taking me?" Mel asked again. The persistent clank of the cuffs told him she was examining them. He didn't have to look. She knew as well as he did there was no way she could free herself. Not unless she carried a key in her bra. Something he doubted, but he had prepared for the possibility anyway by making sure she couldn't reach it if she did have one.

"Just sit back and enjoy the ride, Mel. You're not exactly in a position to do much else."

She pushed at the back of his seat with her feet. Marc leaned forward. She might have gotten a little rusty, but she still packed a hell of a punch. And he wouldn't put it past her to have enough strength in those long legs to send him flying through the windshield.

He should have brought some shackles.

Stick to the plan.

Just because the plan was off course didn't mean he couldn't proceed with the rest of it.

He thought back to a magazine article he'd recently read. When having problems, focus on the good things.

"Mel?" he said quietly.

A long silence, then a tentative, "What?" drifted from the back seat. He looked to find her still examining the cuffs. Marc faced the road again.

"Remember the time we were on the vice-presidential detail in Seattle?"

Silence.

"You remember. He was in Washington for the preprimary debate, and we were placed on extra alert—"

"I remember," Mel interrupted, apparently giving up her study of the cuffs.

He glanced to find her staring at him. "Then you remember what you did when you saw that perp in the hotel kitchen? You wrestled the guy to the floor before he had a chance to identify himself." She turned her face away. "Good thing the vice president's ticker was strong, or you would have given him a heart attack."

No response. Marc tightened his hands on the steering wheel. Maybe that hadn't been the best memory to use.

"Of course you couldn't have known he liked to walk the streets incognito, picking up a paper or two. Hell, none of us knew."

Silence.

Marc cleared his throat. The art of conversation was obviously not an inherited skill. His father was a pro at it— at least with others—as was his brother Mitch. Given Mel's response, he guessed he was still an amateur. "Not in the mood for reminiscing, Mel?"

"Don't call me Mel," she said finally. He exhaled in surprised relief. An angry Mel was much easier to deal with than a silent one. "My name's Melanie. And no, I don't feel like revisiting the past, Marc. I'd just as soon forget it."

He turned onto the on-ramp for I-270 South. "It wasn't that long ago."

"Ninety-two days. Two-thousand, two hundred and eight hours. One hundred, thirty-two thousand—"

"All right, I get the picture already," he grumbled.

"—four hundred and eighty minutes," she finished, her voice little more than a whisper. "That's a lot of time. Enough time for a person to completely reinvent herself." She paused. "I'm not rusty, Marc. I'm not the person you knew."

Maybe she had a point there. Marc rubbed his fingers across his chin. Then again, his reaction to her hadn't changed. While Mel still carried her .25—strapped to her milky thigh, no less—she didn't call herself his partner anymore, in either sense of the word, no matter how much he wanted to lose himself in her. Now more than ever. Three months without Melanie had done that to him.

He resisted the urge to rearrange a certain painfully erect body part into a more comfortable position. He reminded himself that his plan had as much to do with physical urges as it did with the threat that loomed over Mel's head. And the changes in her merely amplified her need for protection.

What would she do when he told her Hooker had escaped from custody en route to his hearing? That it was strongly suspected he was coming after her to finish the job?

He looked at her in the rearview mirror, flinching when the rock she wore on her left ring finger reflected the sunlight. He thought about the velvet pouch in his pocket. His ring was nothing compared to the one she had on. Little more than costume jewelry. Why had he decided an emerald was prettier than a diamond?

He grimaced, wondering why he carried the stupid thing around, anyway.

Marc mulled the situation over for the half-hour ride

into the city, finding no easy answers to his questions or the ones Mel kept asking. Honesty to a degree. That's what a piece in last month's issue of *It's a Woman's World* had said. But what was that degree? He absently thrust his fingers through his hair. Sure, he knew enough not to tell a woman her hips looked big in a certain pair of jeans or that a shade of lipstick looked awful when it did…well, most of the time anyway. But how much did he tell Mel about what was going on? Was it best to keep the truth from her altogether? Was it better to let her believe he'd kidnapped her to keep her from marrying someone else? Which wasn't exactly a lie…

He slid the velvet pouch to the side of his pocket. Who in the hell had colored in so many shades of the truth, anyway? He really couldn't guess how Mel would react. All he knew was that her injury must have scared her but good, or she would have never quit the division.

"God, you're not taking me to your town house, are you?" Mel's voice broke into his thoughts.

He cleared his throat. "So you still recognize the way. Given the number of times you've visited lately, I'm surprised."

She whispered something he couldn't hear. He turned to look at her. He'd noticed before that she'd let her hair grow. He watched the setting sun bounce rays off the golden strands, making it appear as if she wore a halo. Only he knew how much of the devil resided within her, even if she chose to forget.

"What was that?" he asked.

Metal clanked against metal, but she said nothing.

"Let's see, what could it have been? Hmm. Could you have been commenting on how many times I visited you in that colonial mansion wannabe on Cherry Blossom Road in Bedford you now call home?"

Her continued silence told him what he wanted to know.

He grew more agitated. "I was afraid your mother

wouldn't tell you how many times she turned me away—"

"She did not." Another nudge to the back of his seat nearly threw him against the steering wheel. But it was the loud tearing of material that caught his attention.

Marc pulled into the garage of the two-family town house he had lived in for the past ten months. With a flick of the remote, the garage door started to close, clipping off the sunlight. He turned to see Mel's frown as she took stock of the rip in her dress.

"Tsk, tsk," he said softly.

"Go to hell, McCoy."

He climbed out of the Jeep. "Oh, me and hell are coming to know each other very well lately," he said to himself, then opened the back door. "Are you going to cooperate? Or should I leave you out here until you cool down?"

He watched her school her features into a mask of calm. Only the bright spots of red on her cheeks gave away her true feelings. "I'll cooperate."

He grinned, not buying her act for a second. "Good."

He took the key to the cuffs out of his front jeans pocket and released her. She rubbed at the red rings around her wrists, then stared at the tear in her dress.

"I can't believe you did this," she said as she scooted to the door. Marc stepped out of the way. "Where's the phone?"

She glanced around the garage to where a telephone extension had once hung next to the door to the kitchen. "Phone?" he asked.

Her gaze warily shifted to him. "Yes, you know, that little banana-shaped instrument you use to contact others. Where is it?"

He glanced at her, taking in her shoeless feet. "Let's go inside, why don't we?"

He placed his hand at the small of her back, silently groaning at the way the silk of her dress complimented the warm hollow. She didn't budge. "I'm not going anywhere with you."

He cocked an eyebrow. "Oh? You're here, aren't you?"

"Not by choice." She moved away from his touch, and he saw the ten-inch tear in the side seam of her dress.

He dropped his voice an octave, doubt briefly tainting his intentions. "What makes you think you have a choice now?"

Wrong thing to say. He knew without any magazine telling him that. No one liked to be boxed in. Especially a woman like Mel.

He watched as her eyes widened slightly. For the first time in the years he'd known her, he spotted fear lurking in her face, in her stiff posture. Never had Melanie Weber been afraid of him. And he didn't like the thought that she was now, even if it was for her own good. He molded his fingers gently around her upper arm and urged her toward the door.

"Come on. If you're still hungry, you can raid the fridge while I see to some things."

She tried to tug her arm from his grip. "I don't want to raid your fridge, Marc. I'm supposed to be in the middle of a perfectly wonderful dinner with—"

"I know. Your groom-to-be, his parents, your mother and all of Bedford. I hate to tell you this, Mel, but I think your guests have figured out you won't be back."

Her gaze fastened on his face, but she kept walking. He steered her through the door, then closed it and turned the key in the dead bolt. He pocketed the key, then let her go, oddly disappointed he no longer had a reason to touch her.

She ran her hand absently over the marble-tiled countertop that had been the deciding factor in his taking the town house, though he had yet to understand her fascination with the piece of rock. She turned toward him, her eyes soft and watchful.

Marc barely heard the loud, curious meow and the

clicking of nails against the kitchen floor until Brando wound himself around Mel's ankles.

"Oh, God, you still have him." She bent to lift the cat into her arms and cuddled him close. For a moment, a crazy moment, Marc allowed himself to believe Mel was here on her own steam.

"Of course, I kept him," Marc said quietly, turning away. He tensed, half expecting her to mention all the times he swore he'd toss the scruffy scrap of gray fur from the place after she'd dumped the stray in his lap. But after Mel disappeared from his life... Well, the arguments on how the new town house and the cat wouldn't get along meant little. And having something of Mel meant a hell of a lot more.

He felt her probing gaze on him. Well, that bothersome habit hadn't changed, had it? She still looked at him as if she could see to the core of his soul. And, stupidly, he still felt the need to hide it from her. Especially now.

He opened the refrigerator, using the door to block her gaze. "Why don't you go wait in the living room. This shouldn't take long." Peripherally, he saw her finger the empty phone perch on the far kitchen wall. Then the pat of her shoeless feet against the tile told him she had left the room.

MELANIE MADE HER WAY through the all too familiar town house, trying not to notice the changes. Or, more importantly, trying not to register all that hadn't changed.

She didn't want to see the paperback she had readily abandoned on the side table when Marc had tackled her on the leather sofa.

She didn't want to remember how they had a wallpaper glue fight while decorating.

She rested her hand on the dining room table, trying to erase from her mind what had happened the one and only time they had attempted to have a civil meal, only to end up with her right elbow resting in a plate full of mashed potatoes. It had taken three washes to get all the gravy out of her hair.

She closed her eyes. No phones. Not a single one of the three extensions was in sight. She swallowed the panic that had been accumulating in the back of her throat all day. During the drive, she had come to the conclusion that she couldn't return to the dinner and pretend nothing had happened; that much was obvious. But at least she could tell someone she was okay and that they shouldn't worry.

"Who would you like to explain this to, Melanie?" she whispered, absently stroking the purring cat in her arms. "I've got it. You'd call Craig. He'd be upset, but surely he'd understand. No, no, you'd call Mother and make her worry even more that you're going to run out on your groom."

She leaned against the living room wall and closed her eyes, not wanting to be reminded of the past. But everything in this place brought the memories rushing back. Marc hadn't changed a single thing since their breakup. She came awfully close to indulging in a smile, thinking she could check back in fifty years and everything would probably be the same, only a lot older. His battered leather recliner was still a mile away from the television set, though he'd argued with her for weeks after she had convinced him to move it there. Her short-lived plan had been to arrange his things so that when she moved in, he wouldn't have to move anything to accommodate her stuff.

It was a stupid plan.

She swallowed, trying to forget all about that time in her life. Staring at spilt milk wasn't going to get it cleaned up, as her mother was fond of saying.

She thought about Craig and all he offered, comparing him to Marc and the thrilling impermanence of a life spent on the edge. Craig was practical, thoughtful and predictable. Marc was exhilaratingly irresponsible, selfish and boyishly irresistible.

But, ultimately, the absence of a father in her life made Melanie desperately long for her child to know one. And Craig would give her child everything he needed. Her baby deserved that.

Marc... Well, Marc wasn't interested in being a father.

No matter what happened, she knew she had to marry Craig.

Still, the sadness that filled her was overwhelming in its intensity.

As her gaze slowly focused, it settled on the coffee table. A pile of well-thumbed magazines littered the top. Melanie bent down and let Brando go. The cat scampered toward the kitchen, as she moved toward the table.

Cosmopolitan? Redbook? Working Woman? She slowly leafed through the magazines strewn across the surface between empty beer bottles and a doughnut box.

"Mel, I was thinking—" Marc's words abruptly stopped.

Before she had a chance to blink, he was across the room, gathering the books. "Never mind those. They, um, were delivered here by mistake."

Melanie turned over the one she held and found his name on the label. She blinked at him, a curious warmth spreading through her chest.

He jerked the magazine from her grasp.

She decided he had gone mad. He might look like the same hunk who had swept her off her feet two years ago with his charm and devil-may-care take on life. But his actions now... She was afraid they marked him a few croutons short of a full salad. So what if he looked even more in control than he ever had? He had kidnapped her, for God's sake. Swiped her from her wedding rehearsal dinner not ten yards away from a roomful of guests. Threw her over his shoulder and handcuffed her in the back of his Jeep. And he was reading women's magazines. That more than anything proved he wasn't in full charge of his faculties.

Yet the fact that he was reading women's magazines somehow touched her.

"I should have left you handcuffed," Marc grumbled.

"Let me guess, you like the pictures," she said, forcing her gaze to the French doors leading to the back yard. He was so outrageously embarrassed, reminding her of a young boy who'd just got caught with a *Playboy* under his bed. "Actually, I'm surprised you didn't. Leave me handcuffed, that is."

He stuffed the magazines into a garbage can. "I didn't think it was necessary. The way I figure it, you run, I'm on you before you can get ten feet." He tugged at the collar of his T-shirt. "So you might as well sit down until I'm finished." Tin cans clunked together as he tossed a handful into a large brown bag.

She watched him, not sure what to make of his behavior. He was still so much a little boy wrapped up in a gorgeous man's body. On the job he was a confident professional, but when it came to matters of the heart, she was afraid Marc could qualify for the role of Dumbest in the sequel to *Dumb and Dumber*. She swallowed hard. She pushed aside her attraction to those endearing qualities and reminded herself that she needed a responsible adult.

She absently sat in his recliner, but the action wasn't as easy as she had hoped. The hem of her dress hiked up to her panties. She tugged at her sister's idea of a dress, wishing she had gone with something a little more conservative.

"Do you want a coffee? It's your favorite," Marc said.

She shifted to look into his face. He held out a hefty mug to her. The aroma of French vanilla made her mouth water. She accepted the mug, longing for a sip, though she couldn't drink it. Caffeine and all that. Still, she decided it best not to argue with him right now. She'd pretend to drink the coffee. Then she would talk him into letting her go. It was as simple as that.

Marc continued doing whatever it was he was doing, passing through the room several times carrying bags. One bag in particular caught her attention because it wasn't plain brown paper like the others, but rather a glossy pink with purple handles. She squinted to read the words printed across the outside: Old Towne Bed and Bath Shoppe.

She sat upright and made an attempt at pulling the ripped seam of her dress together even as she tugged at the hem. "Okay, let me phrase my question in a way even you can understand, Marc. What, exactly, is your objective?"

"My objective?" He stood and stuffed something into the pink bag.

She fidgeted. "You didn't go through all this just so you could serve me a coffee." She glanced at the untouched coffee in the cup she'd put on the table, then eyed him. "Did you?"

He rocked on his heels, then folded his arms across his chest. "No, you're right, I didn't."

Hope shot through her. He was beginning to sound reasonable. Good. That meant she would soon be out of this place and back to her new safe, predictable life in Bedford in no time. "So?"

"Ah, yes, my objective." He reached to scoop up Brando, who sat on the floor. The casual move made Melanie remember when she'd brought the scrappy cat home from the shelter after having him neutered and declawed. Marc had picked up the tiny, shivering kitten, drew him close to his chest and said, "I coulda been a contender," earning the cat his name.

Marc cleared his throat. "Let's just say it's important for you to spend some time with me, that's all."

"Time?" Melanie focused on the conversation, not liking his vague answer. "How much time are we talking about here? An hour? Two hours?"

He lifted his head to meet her gaze. Melanie's throat closed at the determination she saw in his eyes. "As much time as it takes."

"What?" Melanie rose from the chair. "As much time as it takes for what?" Certainly he wasn't trying to... "I am going to marry Craig, Marc."

He stepped closer to her, then appeared to change his mind and stepped back. Despite the distance that separated them, Melanie felt as if he'd touched her.

"All this, your getting married...it's about that night, isn't it?" he asked.

She knew he had to be talking about the disastrous discussion they'd had about love just before she was shot. Melanie swallowed her surprise. She had seen Marc McCoy in various hair-raising situations. But never had he been so eager to understand.

"It's about more than that night." She fought to hold his gaze, though she wanted to look elsewhere, fearing what she might give away. "Marc, I know my getting married must have come as a shock to you." She tried to feel her way. She didn't know what to say. Especially when he dragged a hand through his dark hair, tousling it in that way she loved. "For Pete's sake, we don't even know each other."

She stopped and looked him in the eye. "I mean, we *know* each other. But not very well." She was faltering and she knew it. There were some areas where they knew each other only too well. "I've never even met your family. You've met my mother, but just the once." She cleared her throat. "I'm not even sure what your favorite color—"

"Green."

She gave a shaky smile. "And mine?"

He stared at her, seemingly at a loss. She wished he would say purple, as if that in itself would prove he cared about her.

But he remained painfully silent.

Finally, he said gruffly, "I'm going to finish up. Why don't we have this little talk later, okay?"

"Talk," Melanie repeated numbly, her point more than hitting home. "Yes, yes, we do need to have a talk."

She watched him set Brando down and leave the room, incapable of all but the simplest of movements. Like blinking.

She desperately needed to convince him that they weren't meant for each other—before his mere presence swayed her the other way. She needed to remind him that he didn't love her, no matter how much it hurt to face that inescapable fact.

Brando brushed against her foot. She absently scooped the tom up and stroked him, then glanced at her watch. She caught herself bouncing the cat as if he were an infant and forced herself to stop. She didn't understand why she had to explain anything. Hadn't it been Marc who said he never wanted children? Hadn't it been Marc who was nowhere to be seen when she was lying in a hospital bed after surgery to remove the bullet she'd taken? When she'd learned she was pregnant?

She realized she was close to tears. She couldn't deal with this right now. She really couldn't.

Her legs were no longer able to support her. She sank into the beige leather couch, listening to the sound of running water from the kitchen. Marc's peculiar behavior wasn't the only cause for concern. There were her curious feelings for the man, reignited the moment she saw him standing outside the inn's ladies' room. She blamed his absence from her life, the shock of seeing him again after so long, for most of her reaction. But she knew she couldn't easily dismiss the other feelings that had stirred to life. Her blood ran thick; her lips were forever dry, as though waiting for him to moisten them with his kiss; her body trembled in a way she had somehow forgotten it could but all too readily remembered.

But it was more than that. She had missed him. Missed his boyish smile, his adolescent sense of humor—

"Are you sure you don't want something to eat before we leave?"

Marc's question pulled her from her thoughts. At the mention of food, the cat leaped from her lap and meowed. Melanie swallowed the lump in her throat. Marc acted as if this situation were nothing more than two old flames catching up, but the fact that he'd carried her there, not to mention removing all the telephones, told her she was little more than a prisoner.

Prisoner.

"Uh, yes, I am a little hungry," she said, trying for a smile. His grin told her he wasn't buying her change in behavior. Still, Melanie tilted her head and desperately kept smiling. Finally he said something under his breath, then returned to the kitchen.

Her heart racing, Melanie got up from the couch so quickly she was sure she heard another rip of fabric somewhere in the back of her dress. She tugged at the hem and hurried toward the French doors—the obvious choice for escape. Too obvious.

"Think, Mel, think." She started at her use of her old nickname. Everyone at the division had called her Mel. Initially, she had encouraged the habit. The male name did away with a lot of the pre-meeting sexual discrimination so inherent on the job, especially since out of two thousand secret service agents, only one hundred twenty-five were women. Of course, it hadn't meant a thing after she met someone face-to-face, but with her knowledge of tactical techniques and natural skill with firearms, she had more than held her own in the male-dominated field.

The bedroom.

She bit her lip. Marc would probably expect the bedroom to be the last place she'd go. Given his ego where his libido was concerned, he would think her too weak to confront the memories of their lovemaking.

She tried the door to the bedroom, then caught sight of the bathroom. She hurried across the hall and turned on both faucets, then pushed the auto lock in and closed the door before stepping into the bedroom.

Twilight filtered through the miniblinds on the windows, slanting intimate shadows across the unmade king-size bed. Melanie swallowed. If Marc had judged her too weak to come in here, she had a sinking feeling he might have been right. They hadn't spent a great deal of time in the town house, but what little time they had was spent primarily in this room.

She edged along the wall and the closed closet doors, irrationally afraid that if she got too close to the familiarly rumpled bed, she might be tempted to climb in. Her pulse racing, she made her way to the closest window. The other one would require her to step around *that* bed. Her palms grew damp, and she hoped she wouldn't have to do that.

"Mel?"

Every molecule of air froze in her lungs as Marc's voice filtered through the closed door. There was a quick knock against the bathroom door across the hall. She hurried to the window. Hoisting the miniblinds, she stared outside, then tried to unlatch the window. It wouldn't budge. She glanced over her shoulder to make sure the door was still closed and blindly tried to open the window. *Nothing.* She stared at the previously easy-to-turn latch and found that a tiny lock had been secured to it. She considered using the brass clock on the night table to break the glass. Then her gaze caught on something else.

Slowly, she lifted the turned-down picture frame next to the clock. Her breath caught when she looked at a picture of herself.

Where? How? Neither of them had ever owned a camera. Heat swept across her cheeks. At least not while they were together. Now she owned a top-of-the-line camera with all the extras in preparation for the birth of her—their—baby.

But this picture...

She scanned the background of the photo and realized she hadn't posed for the shot. It had been taken on the job. Marc must have had a copy made and had her image cropped and enlarged. Her heart gave a tender squeeze.

"Nice try."

Melanie jumped, nearly dropping the picture as she turned toward the door. There was a time not so long ago when no one could have entered a room without her knowing it. Obviously that was no longer the case. She turned to find Marc filling every inch of the doorway, his hands on his lean hips, his sexy grin peeling back the layers of her resistance.

"I..." She what? Melanie swallowed and put the picture frame on the nightstand. She had tried to escape. It was as simple as that. "You can't keep me here, you know. By now a lot of people will be looking for me." She stared at him. "You're well versed on the legalities, so I won't bother with those." She squared her shoulders. "But I don't know if you understand how morally incorrect this is. If you have one ounce of feeling left for me, Marc, you'll let me walk out the front door. Please."

"I have more than an ounce of feeling left for you, Mel. That's why I can't let you go." His expression shifted briefly. "Take it off."

"What?" Melanie's gaze slid to his face. She must have misheard him. Certainly, he wasn't suggesting—

"Take off the dress, Mel."

Her heart started beating double time. Her gaze slid to the rumpled sheets on the bed next to her. Her hands absently stroked her slightly rounded stomach. "Did you hear one word of what I just said?" she asked.

"There's nothing wrong with my hearing."

She fought not to fidget. "No, there probably isn't. Now, your thought processes are a different matter."

Melanie pushed away from the window and strode toward the hall, pretending a bravado she didn't feel. She stopped when she reached the door—and him—but refused to meet his gaze. She focused on his chest instead, then decided that wasn't much safer. "Excuse me, but I think I'd, um, feel better if we moved to the other room."

His eyebrows rose. "You're the one who led me in here."

"Led you?" She looked into his eyes, something she swore she wouldn't do but did anyway. This close, the black of his pupils seemed ready to take over the brown of his eyes. She'd always loved his eyes. "I didn't lead you anywhere." Her thrumming body disagreed. "I was trying to escape. Big difference."

"I can't let you do that."

Melanie wasn't sure what she wanted to do more as hot tears blurred her vision—slug him or cry.

He looked as though she had gone ahead and slugged him, apparently as shocked by her tears as she was.

"I didn't…I mean, that's not…. Oh, hell." Finally, he moved. Just enough to let her into the hall. Except that would mean brushing against him. Not a good idea. Especially since she couldn't seem to control the faucet to her waterworks. *It has to be the hormones.*

Melanie rapidly blinked back the dampness. She had not walked away from Marc McCoy because she had stopped wanting him. She doubted the chemistry that existed between them would ever be completely gone. Neither would their history, considering the child that was even now growing inside her.

She cleared her throat then swept past him, her breasts and hips brushing against him for the briefest moment. Tingles ignited at the points where they touched, then swept throughout her limbs, making her momentarily dizzy. Her ability to go on with her life had depended a great deal on Marc's absence. Now that he had reentered the picture—despite the Neanderthal way in which he had—she had a problem on her hands. Especially if he intended to see through this plan of his to hold her hostage. Melanie held her head straight as she led the way into the living room. Brando was in the middle of the couch, giving himself a thorough bath. Melanie sat fidgeting next to him, rationalizing that if Marc decided to sit next to her, he would have to—

He moved the cat.

Melanie got up from the couch quicker than she thought possible. "I can't believe you're doing this. I don't know what you're trying to prove."

"Take off the dress, Mel," he said in the same exasperated tone he'd used in the bedroom.

"Why?"

He sank to the couch and rested his arms on his knees. "For one, if you keep pulling on that hem you won't have anything left to take off."

Melanie caught herself trying to elongate the length of the dress by sheer will alone. She switched to pulling the tear in the side together. "I always said you were about as romantic as a rock."

"Yeah, well, even a rock knows that dress and the other you plan on wearing on Saturday make you an easy target."

Melanie's throat tightened. Target? Her gaze honed in on his face.

He said something under his breath. "As long as you're wearing that thing, there's a chance you'll try to escape again."

"What did you mean by an easy target?" she asked tightly. "Target for what?"

"You're trying to change the subject, Mel."

She hesitated. Something about the way he said that further unnerved her, and he wasn't meeting her eyes. Whenever he refused to look at her, it meant he was lying. "Marc—"

"Take it off, Mel," he said.

Anger won out over paranoia. "I see. You figure if I'm nearly naked I won't make a run for it."

"Uh-huh."

She swallowed, hating that he looked relieved.

He shrugged, his half-boy, half-rogue grin melting her insides. "If you'd like you can also consider this a form of punishment for trying to escape."

She attacked her hem with renewed vigor. "So now it's a punishment."

He pushed to his feet and rounded the coffee table. "Can you just be quiet for a minute, Mel, and take off the damn dress?"

3

SO MUCH for all the advice he'd picked up. So far he was batting zero for two. Revisit the past, they said. He mentioned Seattle, and she clammed up. Let her know with small gestures how you feel. Mel looked about ready to jump out of her skin.

Marc eased Mel around, the feel of silk and her firm, warm flesh confounding him. In all the thought that had gone into this plan, nowhere had he left room for the riot of emotion that charged him every time he came within smelling distance of Melanie Weber. And now that he was touching her—well, it was better he didn't think about that.

He eyed the back of the dress. "Where's the zipper?"

Mel was so tense he swore her hair trembled. "There is no zipper," she whispered.

She tried to pull away, but he held her. "Yeah, well, if there's a way into this thing, there has to be a way out, right?" He spotted the buttons that stretched from the neck all the way down to her softly rounded rear end. He cleared his throat, his patience dwindling fast.

"I suppose this is a woman's idea of romance," he murmured. He'd read his fill on how to fix a soothing bubble bath and knew what type and color every piece of lingerie meant. Pushing a tiny pink button through a silky loop, he winced at the sight of his callused thumb against the delicate material. He didn't think the editor had him in mind when writing about stuff like this.

The herbal smell of her hair reached his nose, and he battled a groan. Ravishing Mel was no way to protect her.

Or to convince her not to marry the other guy. Yes, he'd missed touching her. But more than that, he'd missed her and everything that was her. Her laugh. Her quiet strength. Her sharp mind and even sharper wit. His thoughts shifted to Tom Hooker and the bullet that had taken all that away from him. The man who even now posed a threat to Mel's life. He chose to ignore that things had gone awry before then.

Suppressing the desire to rip off the ruined dress, Marc tried to make quick work of the buttons, but the closer he got to the small of her back, the quicker his pulse pounded. It usually took a whole lot more than undoing somebody's buttons to arouse him. Then again, Mel had always been able to turn him on with little or no effort. His painfully aroused condition proved that hadn't changed.

That's not why we're here, he reminded himself. Yes, he wanted to take Mel right here and now. On the carpet, on the couch, against the wall. Just like old times. Lose himself in her and forget the past three months. Forget that damn hospital and the battle he'd fought and lost to go in there to see her. Forget that even now, out there somewhere, Hooker was looking for revenge against Mel because she was the one responsible not only for foiling his assassination attempt, but for his arrest.

He suspected, from the trembling of Mel's fingers where she stubbornly held the rip in her dress together, that she wouldn't put up much of a struggle if he pulled her into his arms. He had guessed that the instant he'd met her eyes at that stupid rehearsal dinner. But sex had never been their problem. It wasn't the reason she had left him. And it wasn't the way to bring her back.

Neither is kidnapping her, his conscience taunted.

As each button gave, the material of the dress gaped open, baring her creamy flesh. Marc's jeans tightened uncomfortably. The closer he moved to the arch of her back, the louder the blood roaring in his ears got. Finally all the buttons were undone. He touched her back with his rough fingertips, then drew them down until they rested at the top of her panties.

He absorbed her shiver.

"Please don't," she whispered, breathless.

While she said one thing with her mouth, her body was speaking a whole different language. A language even he could understand. She leaned into his touch and tilted her head to the side, baring her neck to his gaze. One thing he was coming to learn was that no meant no, and that included *don't.* But when her lush rear end pressed against his erection, everything he'd read in the past three months vanished, and he knew nothing more than an urgency to touch Mel in a way he hadn't for a long, long time.

He lowered his mouth to her neck, laving the silky skin there. He circled her rib cage and filled his palms with her breasts. The need that surged through him was almost frightening in its intensity. She whimpered and pressed her bottom against him more insistently. He nearly lost it right then and there.

"Please don't," she whispered again, her face flushed. But this time she moved away, her hands tugging her hem down and uselessly trying to hold the dress together at the back.

Marc's gaze dropped to her mouth. Her lips were slightly parted, her elegant throat trying to swallow. Funny, he had never noticed how long and graceful her neck was. He'd always thought of her as mouthwateringly attractive, but he had never stopped to define by degrees how each part equaled the delicious whole. Outside the bedroom, he'd always thought of her as his equal. Part of that might stem from the fact that they had been partners before lovers, but Marc suspected most of the reason was his own witlessness.

"What are you afraid of, Mel?" he asked, trying to crush the desire threatening to burn right through his veins. "Do you think I can't even unbutton your dress without wanting to jump your bones?"

A shadow of a smile flitted around her eyes, making him want to coax it out. She realized as well as he did how close he'd come to doing just that. "Three months ago you wouldn't have gotten past the third button."

"Three months ago I was a different man," he said, using her words against her. She backed up toward the couch, uncertainty on her face.

He cleared his throat. "Aren't you forgetting something?"

She stared at him blankly, color still high on her cheeks.

"The dress."

"You're serious, aren't you?"

"Uh-huh."

Something flashed in her eyes, reminding him of the Mel he had always admired. The one who never passed up a challenge, a person who could play the I-dare-you game just as well, and often better, than the guys. Her gaze never leaving his, she tugged at the material, pulling first one, then the other, sleeve free. Then with an expression that seemed to ask him, "What do you think of that?" she released her grip, and the dress glided to the floor in a shallow puddle of pink silk.

She stood in front of him, arms stiffly at her sides, nothing but a strapless strip of material covering her breasts and a tiny scrap of triangular silk barely concealing the hair between her legs. Marc's throat closed as his gaze followed the toned line of her inner thigh down to her sexy feet. It took everything he had not to drag her into his arms. All she needed was that pair of stiletto heels he'd tossed in the back of the Jeep, and she would be every man's idea of a dream come true. Problem was, she already was his dream. Even with the scar he couldn't bring himself to look at somewhere above her bra line.

"Impressive," he said, vaguely registering that his voice still worked. "Tell me, Mel, will The Fool appreciate your effort to make sure the wedding night is something to remember? Or has he already tasted the sweets in the candy store?"

The redness in her cheeks told him he'd said the wrong thing...again. Marc bit back a curse, watching as she quickly bent to pull the dress on.

"Trust you to make everything sound dirty. And his name is not The Fool. It's Craig."

He roughly caught her hands. "Has he, Mel?"

He'd told himself countless times it didn't matter if Mel had slept with another man. In fact, he had already accepted that she probably had. But seeing her nearly naked, the slightly rounded muscles of her stomach drawn taut, her womanhood so proudly accentuated by the naughty panties, shot his efforts all to hell. He was back to square one, back to when he had wallowed in a jealous funk at the thought of another man touching her.

She glanced away. "What does it matter?"

He forced her to look at him, aware he was being rougher than necessary but unable to help himself. "Answer me, Mel. Have you slept with him?"

She met his gaze, the moisture in her eyes despite the courageous way she held her head nearly knocking him over. She said nothing for a long moment, merely stared at him in that unblinking way that always drove him crazy. Then she lowered her lashes and looked at the dress pooled around her feet. "Not that it's any of your business, but...no. I haven't slept with him."

She said the words so quietly, Marc wasn't certain he had heard her. But the relief that eased through his tense muscles told him all he needed to know. What he had suspected. What he had hoped.

She hadn't been able to be with anyone else, either. Good.

Of course it did little to solve that other little problem. The fact that she was still getting married.

He couldn't help grinning. "Do you remember the first

time we went to that hot dog place down on Mission? The one with those old-fashioned mustard bottles?"

She tugged herself free of his grasp. "This is stupid."

She reached for the dress again. He established his hold. "Oh, no, you don't." She fought him, this time with the strength that had made her one of the best in the business. "I told you the dress comes off, and it stays off until we leave."

"What kind of game are you playing, Marc?" she asked hoarsely, the ragged emotion in her voice like a punch to the gut.

He nearly let her go.

"It's no game, Mel. It's punishment, remember?" His gaze flicked over her flushed skin. "You tried to escape, and now you're facing the consequences."

"So you just expect me to sit around here for how ever long you decide...." She hesitated. "Butt naked?"

Marc's grin widened. "Not butt naked, Mel. At least not if you behave yourself."

She moved her head in a way that flipped her hair over her shoulder. And oh, what a shoulder it was, too. At least the part he allowed himself to view. The other side and the scar that loomed in his peripheral vision remained untouched by his direct gaze. "So what do I have to do to get my...clothes back?"

A dozen, impossible, improbable ideas sprang to mind. "Oh, I don't know. I suppose we could work out some sort of merit system." He thought for a moment. "Tell you what. You cooperate with what I have in mind, and I'll award you points."

"Points?" The wariness was back in her eyes. "What kind of points?"

He sighed. "Not the type you're thinking. And here we thought I was the one with the dirty mind." He released her wrists, then reached for the dress. She quickly stepped out of it, and he tossed it to a dining room chair behind him. "I may have sunk to kidnapping, but I'm no rapist."

"That's a relief."

Though she tried for sarcasm, her tone fell just shy of the mark. "Is it, Mel? Could it be true that you haven't thought about us at all?"

She was silent. Marc found it incredible that he was standing in front of a half-naked Mel and had no urge to look past her face for the answers he might find there.

"Is this one of the questions that will earn me points?"

"No," he said, his frustration building. "This is one of the questions that will help me figure out where I went wrong."

Mel stilled, staring at him in a way he couldn't interpret.

The mechanical din of "One Hundred Bottles of Beer on the Wall"—the tune that served as his doorbell—echoed through the town house. They both stood completely still until it rang again.

"Seems we have a visitor," she said quietly.

Marc glanced toward the door, then crossed his arms. "I have a visitor. You're marrying someone else in two days, remember?"

Which, now that he could think about it with objectivity, didn't make any sense at all. He grimaced. He hadn't been the only one not interested in marriage. Going into any relationship, he was usually the one worried about the woman's intentions after intimacy. But Mel had made it clear the first night they nearly tore each other's clothes off that she wasn't interested in picket fences.

Why, then, was she getting married?

Oh, hell. While she still had a lot of fight in her, Marc watched a lone tear slide down her cheek. She sighed and rolled her eyes toward the ceiling, apparently not liking the display of emotion any more than he did. "Oh, I remember, all right. I think you're the one having trouble with your memory."

Marc shifted uneasily, tempted to give up the whole thing right there and then.

But he couldn't. Not yet. He'd never failed in an assignment, and he wasn't going to start now.

Marc moved toward the front windows and pushed the curtain aside. He grimaced when he spotted the familiar red sports car parked at the curb. *Roger.*

"I'll be back in a minute," he said under his breath. "Don't go anywhere."

Her stare told him she didn't appreciate his attempt at humor.

Marc walked to the door and opened it, frowning at the partner assigned to him a week after Mel left the division…and him.

"What's up, Rog?"

"Oh, not much with me. I'm wondering why you didn't show for work detail this morning, though."

Roger Westfield tried to look around Marc into the town house. Marc made it difficult. Easy to do, considering Roger was at a disadvantage on the doorstep. His thirty-something face was annoyingly handsome, but it was his sharp blue eyes that betrayed exactly how capable he was. Like Marc, he'd never been married, never came close, and he'd been a good partner so far. Marc hadn't taken any points off because Roger had been partners with Hooker when Mel had stumbled on to her would-be assassin's moonlighting endeavors. Too bad Roger was screwing up Marc's good impression of him.

Roger's gaze settled on something inside the town house, then he looked directly at Marc. "You went and did it, didn't you?"

Marc glanced at Mel, where she stood in the middle of the living room, stubbornly making no attempt to cover herself. He pushed Roger outside, then stepped out, leaving the door slightly open so he could keep an ear out for Mel's movements. He wouldn't put it past her to whack

him in the back of his head with a lamp and leave him for
dead.

And he wouldn't put it past Roger to let her walk right
out of the town house and into the line of fire.

Marc thrust his hand through his already disheveled
hair. "I knew I never should have said anything to you."
Actually, he'd had little choice in the matter. The night before last, after the bulletin went out on Hooker's escape,
Roger and he had gone out for a beer. After one too many,
Roger had shared the nasty details of his close calls with
women…and Marc had spilled his guts about what had
happened between him and Mel, including his half-baked
plan to take her into what he saw as protective custody.

This morning a report went out on Hooker's surfacing
in the area, and the whole department had been put on
alert. And Marc had decided to put his plan into action.

Roger said, "You're right. You shouldn't have told me.
But since you did, and I know you used your training to
take that woman in there against her will—" He stopped
abruptly. "Have you lost your mind, McCoy? Do you
know what will happen if she presses charges? I won't
say anything about your job, but the legal—"

"She won't press charges."

Roger frowned. "Excuse me for saying so, buddy, but it
doesn't look like Melanie Weber is a very happy camper
right now."

Like he needed to be told *that*. "What's up, Roger? I
know you didn't come here to offer emotional support."

"Emotional support? You've been reading those
damned magazines again, haven't you?"

Marc stiffened, not about to respond to the question.
When Mel had taken that bullet, then disappeared from
his life, he'd tried everything to figure out exactly how to
make things right with her. And that included reading
those damned magazines, as Roger had an irritating habit
of referring to them. He jammed his fingers through his
hair. In all honesty, he thought a few of the articles di-

rectly addressed exactly where he'd gone wrong with Mel.

Then he'd bought that stupid ring that even now was a leaden weight in his pocket.

"Look, you're right." Roger nodded. "I didn't come by to badger you about your personal business. It's your life, feel free to screw it up."

"Gee, thanks."

"Don't mention it." Roger tried to look through the crack in the door. "Just thought you might like to know a certain somebody's mother contacted our boss demanding an address for you." Marc stared at him. "She was calling from a sheriff's office somewhere in Maryland."

Adrenaline rushed through Marc's body, thick and all-consuming. "Damn, I've got to get her out of here—"

"Whoa, hold on to your shorts there, cowboy. I know your heart is in the right place, but don't you think it would be a good idea to just let her go and let the division protect her?"

What Roger left out was that the division wouldn't give her the protection she needed until after Hooker squeezed off another potshot.

Marc thrust his hand through his hair again. "You'll have to cover for me."

Roger shook his head. "No can do. When the shit hits the fan, that little lady in there is going to tell everyone and his brother I was here. You can put your own ass on the line, but keep your hands off mine."

"I can't let her go," Marc muttered. "Hooker is out there right now, possibly casing Mel's every move. I can't allow him to target her again. I won't."

Why couldn't his plan have gone off without a hitch? Why'd he have to lock her mother in the ladies' john and spill his guts to Roger?

Roger broke into his thoughts. "Come on, McCoy. You don't know that Hooker has her on his shortlist. His emergence in the area could mean he wants to take another shot at the senator."

"Come on, Roger, you know as well as I do that Hooker's cell mate let spill that Hooker planned to seek Mel out. Then there are those letters he sent and all those calls Mel reported to the U.S. attorney's office."

Marc stared at his new partner, feeling ill at ease but unable to describe exactly why. "Just sit on what you know for as long as you can, okay? Long enough for me to get her out of Dodge."

Roger shook his head. "I think you're making a big mistake here. She left you and is about to marry someone else. She's not your responsibility. What's it going to take to get that through your thick head?"

Marc resisted the urge to grab Roger by his neatly starched collar. "Excuse me if I don't take advice from a man who calls a one-nighter a relationship."

"Ouch. This from a guy who thinks *love* is a dirty word." Roger turned and started walking toward his car. "Good luck, buddy. You're going to need it."

Marc stepped inside the town house and slammed the door, causing it to shake on its hinges. What in the hell had Roger meant about *love* being a dirty word?

It was then he realized Mel's dress was no longer draped over the dining room chair...and Mel wasn't there, either.

MELANIE'S SKIN felt hot, and the yearning just a couple of Marc's innocuous touches had awakened threaded through her in an endless ribbon of need. That he had kidnapped her at all should have been motivation enough for her to want to escape. Strangely enough, it wasn't. It was the earnest reaction of her traitorous, hormone-ridden body moments before, as he had slowly, awkwardly unbuttoned her dress, the feel of his slick mouth pressed against her skin that had rocketed her moderate desire to get home to an urgent need to get as far away from Marc McCoy as quickly as possibly.

Even now, she wanted to press her fingers against her unkissed lips, to satisfy the tickle of wanting there that had gone unsatisfied. Instead, she held the doubled-up towel against the bedroom window and carefully tapped it with the brass clock.

Melanie cringed. The sound of breaking glass was louder than she expected as the pieces fell onto the tiled patio outside. Ignoring her thudding heartbeat and the urge to take a moment to see if Marc had heard her, she quickly pulled out the remaining shards, then folded the towel over the sill.

It wasn't a long drop. Maybe only five feet or so. If she lowered herself carefully, there wouldn't be any drop at all. No risk of hurting the baby. Still, that didn't ease the knot of fear that had remained with her since the night…

She drew in a deep breath and tried to swing her leg up, but her dress forbade the movement. Hiking the skirt up to her hips, she ignored the irony and swung her leg over the sill. Had she been thinking straight, she would have grabbed a T-shirt and a pair of sweats from Marc's drawers.

But she didn't have time now. She had no idea how long Marc planned to talk to his visitor—God, was Roger Westfield really his new partner?—but she didn't gather it would be long. Her leg slipped, and she grabbed onto the wood window molding for dear life. Taking long, measured breaths, she leveraged her other leg through the window, her edginess having more to do with her still raging hormones than concern about getting caught.

Okay. Now all she had to do was turn around and with the strength of her hands and arms, lower herself down.

Easier said than done.

Inside the town house she heard the slamming of a door. Her heart threatened to leap from her chest. Right this minute Marc was probably rushing toward the bedroom. She quickly maneuvered her body around and through the window, her gaze cemented to the closed bedroom door. It remained closed. In one arm-testing move she lowered her feet to the ground, cringing when glass bit at her stocking feet. But she didn't care. What were a few scrapes and ruined panty hose compared to having her heart broken all over again?

She turned and ran straight into Marc's chest for the second time that day.

4

DESPITE HER THWARTED escape attempt, Melanie was thrillingly aware of every inch of Marc that brushed against her. Her heart beat an uneven cadence in her chest that had little to do with the exertion of climbing from the window and more to do with the irrational hunger she felt for him. The type of craving that did crazy things to her head and made her body hum. The kind of need that had made her press her backside against him minutes before. The sort of irrational yearning for him to be the man she needed right now.

"God, Mel, you're killing me here," he said hoarsely, his fingers clutching her hips not quite against his, but not pushing her away, either.

She swallowed hard, wondering just who was doing the killing when she could feel every glorious inch of him crowded against her stomach.

He groaned and set her firmly away from him. "I take it you're ready to go."

The overdose of hormones combined with sexual frustration made her want to sock him in the nose. She settled for whacking his arm with her open hand.

"Oh, I'm ready to go all right. Home. My home. Now." *Before I do something stupid like make love with you.*

Marc's fingers curled around her chafed wrists, eliciting a shiver. "Sorry, Mel, but that's not an option."

The somber, almost regretful way he said the words made her uneasy. "It is if you let it be."

He said nothing, but the bemused expression left his

face. Melanie fought to keep her gaze locked on him, though she wanted to look away.

"Where are we going, then?"

"Somewhere safe."

All at once, the details of the past hour clicked off in her head. Marc saying they wouldn't be staying at the town house long. His haphazard packing. The visit from his new partner, Roger Westfield. She felt the pounding of her pulse where Marc still held her wrist, remembering the ominous words she caught of Marc's conversation with Roger before she slipped into the bedroom and out the window.

Hooker had escaped.

She felt suddenly faint. That meant Hooker hadn't called her from jail that morning, as she'd assumed... He'd already been out.

"Okay."

One of Marc's eyebrows rose. "Okay?"

Melanie's throat seemed unbearably tight, but she managed a smile. "Yes. Okay."

He instantly released his grip. "After you."

Walking with as much dignity as she could muster, given her torn dress and thwarted escape attempt, Melanie led the way to the French doors and waited patiently as he unlocked and opened them.

SHE KNOWS. Marc admitted he might be a little dense when it came to relationships, but he knew Mel. He took the cat carrier from her and put it into the back of the Jeep. Her new awareness didn't manifest itself in the obvious way. No. She was far from demanding an explanation, but her acquiescence was more unsettling. There was a worried tension around her mouth, and her movements were stiff and awkward. Her only demand was that they take Brando with them when he had been about to pour a hefty amount of food out for the old, fat tom.

Damn. She must have overheard his conversation with

Roger. Sure, he knew he'd have to spill the beans sooner or later and let her in on the reason he had swiped her outside the john at her own wedding rehearsal dinner. But he'd planned to play his cards close to his chest at least until he could figure out a way to break the news to her gently.

He eyed the way she nervously pulled at the tear in her dress and tried to reassure Brando, who was meowing up a storm in the carrier. Her skirt-pulling wasn't nervous in the way it had been earlier, when he suspected her intention was a vain wish to keep him from sneaking a peek. No. Mel looked ready to jump right out of her skin. And that bothered him.

Before he could stop himself, he brushed his knuckles against her cheek. "You all right?"

The worry vanished from her green eyes an instant too late. "Sure, I'm fine. Considering I've been kidnapped by a madman."

He grinned at her feeble attempt at humor. *This* Mel he could deal with, even if she wasn't running at full speed. He reached for the cuffs in his pocket.

Mel eyed him. "Don't tell me you're going to shackle me up again."

Marc fingered the cool, heavy metal. "Given your new habit of creating an exit where one wasn't meant to exit, I think it's a pretty good idea, don't you?"

"Trust me, I'm not about to go jumping out of a moving vehicle."

"No?"

"No."

"I'd really like to take your word for it, Mel, but considering we both had the same training, and I figure you're at least as good as I am at rolling out of a moving car..." Marc placed one of the cuffs around her left wrist. She yanked on it angrily.

"Pig."

"Mule."

He hustled her toward the driver's door. Only when her back was turned did he attach the other cuff to his right wrist. Mel tugged.

"Watch it, will you," he grumbled. "I'm attached to that arm."

She swung around, glaring when she saw what he'd done.

"Get in the Jeep, Mel."

She yanked on the cuffs again and smiled at his scowl. "Doesn't feel so hot when the cuff's on the other hand, does it?"

"Bite me, Mel. Now get in."

When she continued to hesitate, he maneuvered her around and boosted her up, his palms blessedly full of her sweet behind. She squeaked, and he gave her delectable cheeks a good squeeze, liking that he still knew some of her buttons to push. She immediately scrambled inside and over to the passenger seat, nearly taking his hand off in the process.

"I don't know what you hope to accomplish by acting like a cad," she said, giving the cuffs a tug for emphasis after he was in the Jeep.

I hope to keep you at arm's length, Marc thought, tugging her hand so he could turn the ignition. He needed to keep his wits about him now that they were going into the open. More patrols looking for him meant fewer on Hooker's trail. "Hey, can't blame a guy for taking advantage of an especially advantageous situation, can you?"

Mel turned toward the window and whispered something under her breath.

"I'm over here, Mel."

"I'm very clear on where you are, Marc. At least physically."

He grimaced, wishing the tightness of his jeans away. She didn't have any idea about his physical position.

"So, tell me," she said, her voice dropping an octave, "how long have you and Westfield been partners?"

He shrugged, but didn't feel any of the nonchalance the action indicated. Not when she'd been lying in a hospital bed recovering from a bullet wound that had nearly taken her life. "A week after Hooker was arrested."

"Oh." She turned away again, but this time she spoke loud enough for him to hear her. "How are you two getting along?"

Not as good as you and I did. "Fine. He can grind on a guy's nerves after a while, but otherwise he's on the ball."

Her smile caught him off guard.

"What?"

She shook her head. "Nothing."

He hated when she did that.

She sighed. "I was just wondering if there's anyone out there who's capable of *not* grinding on your nerves."

He looked at her squarely. "You were okay."

"Oh, no, I wasn't. At least not in your book."

He frowned. Mel was the best damned partner he'd ever worked detail with. Didn't she know that? She pulled at her short dress again, jerking his hand in her direction. He guessed she didn't have a clue how he really felt. "I thought we were pretty good together."

"At least up until the point where I nearly got myself killed."

Marc shifted his fingers the fraction of an inch needed to cup her knee. He was frustrated by the stockings that separated her skin from his. "What happened to you could have happened to anyone, Mel. You were doing your job." *And if I had been doing mine, I would have taken that damned bullet for you.*

Her gaze was unwavering. "Where in the job description does it say I have to take down one of our own?"

"Hooker stopped being one of our own the minute he shot at the senator."

Marc's fingers stilled on her knee, and the silence stretched. She turned her engagement ring around and around on her finger.

"Did I ever tell you Hooker and I trained together at VMI?" He shook his head, recalling how green he'd been back then. A regular know-it-all and do-it-all who took crap from no one.

He sensed rather than saw Mel's gaze on him.

"One night after really tying one on with some of the guys, it was Hooker who saved my ass." He remembered how he'd tried to take the other, smaller man on after Hooker had told him and the others to cool it. It might have been because of his compromised condition, but quicker than he'd been able to blink, Hooker had pinned him to the ground and told him there was going to be a surprise midnight inspection and he was too damn good a candidate to screw things up now.

Marc realized he'd never thanked Hooker for straightening him up. Two of the guys he'd been with had been booted out that night, no questions asked.

He grimaced, thinking it really didn't matter now. "I never would have thought him capable of something like this. I guess a lot can change about a person in eleven years, huh?"

"A lot can change about a person in three months," Mel said softly.

"You can say that again," he answered just as quietly.

Her .25 was in the glove compartment, where he'd put it. He decided not to worry about it since she didn't seem too intent on escaping anymore.

"Look, Mel, I put off telling you about Hooker because I didn't want to scare you. But I do think it's a good idea if we talk straight now." She nodded, but averted her gaze. "I don't know how much you heard back there, but Hooker told his cell mate he was coming after you."

He watched her swallow.

"So far we have reports of clothes stolen from a clothesline at one place, firearms taken from another, both houses just outside D.C., not too far from here."

She looked at him, her eyes round.

"There, I said it."

A charged silence fell between them as they racked up the miles.

"Thanks," she said softly. "You know, for telling me everything."

He gripped the steering wheel more tightly. "No problem."

He felt her gaze on him again, probing, seeking out chinks in his armor. He rubbed his chin against his shoulder, wondering how the conversation had gotten so serious so fast. And how, exactly, he could steer it back to safer territory.

"Where are we going?" she asked.

Marc studied the highway with exaggerated interest. He thought they'd passed a milestone, but he couldn't be sure. "You'll find out soon enough," he said, preoccupied.

He moved to rub his palm against his jeans, accidentally dragging her hand along for the ride. She gasped when she found her fingers within inches of his zipper. A car horn pierced the air, and Marc realized he'd veered into the next lane. The Jeep nearly went on two wheels as he quickly made the needed correction.

If he didn't watch it, he wouldn't have to worry about Hooker's intentions because both he and Mel would be out of the picture.

"I see your driving hasn't improved much."

The chuckle that vibrated in his chest released some of the tension. "Yeah, well, if I recall, you're not much better behind the wheel."

"Guess that's why neither of us had been given driving detail, huh?"

He briefly locked gazes with Mel, grateful for her tactful ability to drain the stress out of any situation. He supposed it was a gift of sorts, the way she wrapped things up neatly and put them aside. If only that same gift hadn't allowed her to neatly box him up and put him in the closet of her past so easily.

Marc moved to rub his neck, but the clanking of the cuffs told him he'd better not. Instead, he laid his clenched hand on the seat between them, inexplicably irritated by the careful lengths to which Mel went to avoid touching him.

He thoroughly searched the road in front of and behind the Jeep, keeping an eye out for local and state police. The last thing he needed was another monkey wrench thrown into his plans.

THE HANDCUFF around Melanie's wrist felt strangely heavy. Not so much physically, although the metal was hard and unyielding. The peculiar sensation that made her acutely aware of her shallow breathing stemmed more from the symbolism of being attached to Marc than anything else. A physical depiction of what she'd felt mentally for the past three months.

She brushed errant tendrils of hair from her face with her free hand, admitting she'd been wrong to think the baby was the cause of any unfinished business between her and Marc. The truth was that without closure, she may as well be chained to Marc when she walked down the aisle in two days. There was still so much between them. Unresolved emotions. Sizzling tension that arced between them like a visible electrical current. She was aware of his every movement, every tap of his index finger against the steering wheel. Every flex of his thigh muscles as he accelerated or slowed to match highway traffic. Erotically aware of the snug fit of his black jeans across his groin.

Catching her bottom lip between her teeth, she turned to the window, watching the city quickly give way to the lush greenery of the country. But it was the low heat in her lower regions, and not the roadside, that got the bulk of her attention.

Aside from brotherly goodnight kisses, she'd never shared physical closeness with Craig. She'd told herself it didn't matter. Her failed relationship with Marc was an example of why relationships based solely on physical attraction were doomed for failure. But though nothing but a short chain connected her and Marc, she felt his presence more strongly than a physical touch. She was aware of the dampness between her thighs and the involuntary, sporadic tightening of her thigh muscles that caused shivers to shimmy up her stomach and her breasts to swell.

She closed her eyes and dragged in a deep breath. It wasn't fair. How could she still want Marc so much with her body, yet know with her mind that he wasn't the man with whom she could share forever? With whom she could raise her child in a stable, loving environment that included two parents?

She slowly opened her eyes. She'd be better off focusing on where Marc was taking her rather than trying to rehash all the details that led to their breakup.

Breakup. Now there was a word. Had she and Marc really broken up? Not in the traditional sense. They'd had that heated discussion about love that had broken her heart, but there had been no vocal parting. Rather their relationship had suddenly ceased. She'd gotten shot, found out she was pregnant. Her mother had taken over, and Marc had disappeared from her life.

"Hang in there, Mel, it isn't much farther."

She slid her gaze toward Marc, blinking at the familiar words. He'd said exactly the same thing when she was in the ambulance, with him bending over her and smoothing her hair from her face.

"What?" she whispered.

He eyed her closely. "You look like you just saw a ghost."

Maybe it was because she had.

Until that moment she'd completely forgotten the snatches of consciousness between the time when she'd

first spotted Hooker to when she'd been hit in the chest.
She'd felt her knees give out, one by one, then she'd
slumped to the ground. She couldn't remember anything
in one uninterrupted piece after that, only in snatches.
And in every snatch there was Marc's boyishly handsome
face creased in anger and concern just inches above hers.

Melanie tugged at the hem of her skirt, then stopped
when she found Marc's hand resting on her knee. She
looked at his well-shaped fingers and the way they
curved just so against her skin. Then, afraid of reawak-
ening the deep well of feelings for him, she removed
those same fingers from her too hot flesh and laid his
hand firmly on the seat between them.

"Not my fault," he said, giving her a full-wattage Marc-
the-irresistible-playboy grin.

She trained her gaze out the window. "Nothing ever is,
is it, Marc?" she whispered, unsure if he heard her, if it really mattered.

5

MARC CURSED the absence of the moon as he blindly tried to insert the key into the lock. Mel stood beside him, but she was apparently trying to make out where the waters of the Potomac lapped against the shore. Dusk had settled completely, and aside from what little light the multitude of stars provided, they were enclosed in darkness.

"Do some investing?" Mel asked.

The key finally hit home. With a quiet whoosh, he pushed the door open, then eased her inside. "My brother Connor loaned me the place." Which was as much as she needed to know. He closed the door, then searched for a light switch. When a naked bulb in the cracked ceiling fixture illuminated dingy walls, a threadbare plaid couch, a scarred coffee table and little else, he grimaced.

"Charming," Mel whispered.

This certainly wasn't going to earn him any points. "I didn't exactly have time to scope out the place, Mel," he said, inexplicably irritated. In fact, he was lucky to have found the remote cabin on the shores of the Potomac. All he'd been going on was a brief conversation he'd had with Connor, who'd stashed a federal witness there before trial about six months ago. Marc had lifted the keys from his brother's pocket that morning after verifying the cabin was empty.

Mel yanked on the cuff, nearly pulling him over. She smiled at him innocently.

"Is that your not so subtle way of telling me you want loose?"

He fished the key from his jeans pocket and released his side. He pocketed the key.

"Oh, come on, Marc. You're not going to leave these things on me, are you?"

"I haven't decided yet." He spotted a radiator on the far side of the room.

"No, you don't." Mel began backing away from him. "Don't even think—"

The catching of the metal teeth sounded unusually loud in the quiet room as Marc fastened the free cuff to the radiator pipe.

"Just for a minute, I swear." He wanted to go out and check the place to make sure it was as effective at keeping someone in as it was at keeping unwanted people out. He stepped toward the door, not about to fool himself into thinking that darkness and unfamiliarity with the area would keep Mel inside.

"WHEN I GET OUT OF THIS MESS, I'm going to…"

Melanie's words broke off. What would she do? Have her baby's father thrown in jail? She shivered, briefly giving in to the urge to smooth her palm down her stomach. She closed her eyes, amazed that such a small move always managed to calm her, remind her that no matter what was happening, there was something more important she should be thinking about.

No, she wouldn't, couldn't have Marc arrested, the big dummy. His heart was in the right place—he only wanted to protect her. Besides, despite everything that had happened in the past few hours, she was quietly coming to admit that with Hooker on the loose, there was no physically safer place on earth than right here with Marc McCoy.

The safety of her heart, though, was another matter entirely.

She stared at her engagement ring. It flashed, reminding her of a completely different flash of light. A flash that had momentarily blinded her. The night that had changed everything raced through her mind. Her throat tightened, her lungs ached, and a deep sense of loneliness saturated her.

She couldn't remember exactly what had alerted her to the seriousness of the situation when she pulled up to Senator Turow's house. It could have been the all-encompassing silence. Or the fact that no one was where they should have been. Or both, with a generous pinch of gut instinct that told her something was wrong. One minute she and Marc were running a simple errand to see if Hooker or Westfield had found the watch she'd lost earlier in the day, the only thing she had left of her father. The next, chaos erupted.

Melanie forced a swallow through her dry throat. Funny thing was, there had been nothing especially urgent about the detail. Your run-of-the-mill watch of a senator who had declared his candidacy for president. And he wasn't a particularly controversial candidate. No hate groups out there with his name at the top of their political hit list. No ex-wives with a bitter ax to grind. Just a normal, everyday guy who happened to make his career in politics and had made himself an unwitting target. But not a target for a right-wing fanatic. Rather he'd been targeted by one of his own.

Well, one of his own secret service personnel anyway. It was never determined who, if anyone, had been pulling the strings behind the scenes.

The cuffs clanged against the pipe. Melanie looked down to find her fingers absently tracing the scar that lay below the patterned material of her dress. She dropped her hand to her side and gave a ragged sigh. Would there come a time when she wouldn't remember that night with such vivid clarity? When she wouldn't awaken in a cold sweat, her heart beating loudly in her ears, Marc's name on her lips?

"All clear."

The relief that swept through her was frightening merely because it existed at all. "Think of the devil," she whispered as he closed and bolted the door.

"What was that?"

She tried for a smile. "I said, 'You're back.' Now are you going to take these things off or not?"

He appeared to consider the question, but was watching her a little too closely for comfort.

She gave up on the smile and shifted from foot to foot. "Knock it off, Marc. I'm not going anywhere, and you know it."

"How would I know that?" He took the key from his pocket and opened the cuff.

Melanie wiped her damp palms against her dress and rubbed her wrist. "Because we both know there's no safe place for me until Hooker is caught."

His complete and utter stillness riveted her gaze to his face. Never had she known Marc to be completely still outside work. During the long hours spent on detail, he could stand as still as stone, but even then the energy about him fairly pulsed. Now, his stillness transcended the physical, going deeper than she had ever witnessed. His eyes held a calm watchfulness, an understanding, a respect that made her swallow with some difficulty.

An electronic chirp cracked the tension. Melanie blinked as Marc slid a cell phone from inside his vest. *He's had a phone all along.*

"Hello?" He turned away from her, holding the slender receiver to his ear. "Hi, Roger. No word, huh?... No, we're in a safe place.... I don't think it's a good idea to tell you where." He paced a short way and lowered his voice. "Call me the instant you hear anything. And I mean anything."

He closed the phone and slid it into his vest pocket. He turned to her. She wasn't sure what he saw but was surprised when he lifted his hand, skimming the back of his knuckles over her cheek.

"I'm going to get you through this in one piece, Mel."

She resisted the incredible urge to lean into his touch, to give herself over to the turbulent emotions swirling through her bloodstream. The desire that made her want to lose herself in the consuming sensations that came only when loving Marc. "As long as Hooker is out there, no one I know is safe if I'm around them. You know that, don't you?"

"Including me?"

"Especially you."

His halfhearted smile tugged at her heartstrings.

"Seems to me I've already made my decision in that regard."

"Yes, I guess you have." She searched his face. "The question is why? Why after all that's happened are you putting your life on the line for me?"

Now there's a question. Marc had expected many questions, many approaches from Mel, but this hadn't been one of them. What had happened to the spitfire he left cuffed to the cold radiator? The woman out for blood— namely his?

He grimaced, wondering if this was a new approach. A new tactic meant to catch him off guard and create a gaping opportunity for escape. But he'd never known Mel to be very good at deception. When she was mad, she showed it. Boy, did she ever show it.

No, this question had nothing to do with manipulation. She genuinely wanted to know the answer.

If only he had one to give to her.

He withdrew his hand and stalked toward the window. "Guess I don't have to ask if there's an air conditioner in this place." He hoisted open the paint-encrusted window and gave the bars outside a shake to insure they were indeed solid. While the safe house didn't have much in the way of creature comforts, it *was* safe.

"Marc?"

He stepped to a rusted old fan in the corner, checked to

make sure it was plugged in, then turned it on. It wheezed to life, oscillating ineffectively.

"What?" he said finally.

"Why?"

He turned toward her, not feeling much better now that ten feet of dusty wood floor separated them. "Isn't it enough that we used to be partners?"

Her sexy smile was spiced with a bit of challenge. "Somehow I can't see you kidnapping Roger in order to protect him."

"Yeah, well, I didn't used to sleep with Roger, either." Marc saw her wince. *You have a great way with words, Mc-Coy.*

He plucked the decrepit fan from the floor and moved it to the coffee table, yanking out the cord in the process. Cursing, he moved the table closer to the electrical outlet. Still, the infernal contraption blew in every direction but where he wanted it to. "I thought we both agreed that you're now here by choice."

"Well, not quite by choice. But at least I understand the situation a little better." She crossed her arms. Marc's gaze followed the movement, appreciating the way the material of her destroyed dress pulled tight over her breasts. At least she wasn't yanking at the hem anymore.

He strode toward the door.

She quickly followed him, then stopped. "Where are you going?"

He eyed her. She looked altogether too nervous, too vulnerable. "Out to the Jeep to get Brando and the other stuff."

"Oh." Everything about her seemed to relax. What had she thought? That he was going to leave her here by herself? He narrowed his gaze on her face. She hadn't looked exactly right since he'd come into the house. What had happened when he was outside? Had something spooked her?

He rubbed the back of his neck, not knowing quite what to make of the situation. Nothing ever spooked Mel.

You only left the woman handcuffed to a radiator, alone, with no chance for escape while a madman is somewhere out there, after her, his conscience taunted. That would be enough to spook anyone.

He cleared his throat. "But there's no hurry. I could sure use a cup of coffee first."

MELANIE WAS only too happy to see to the coffee and insisted Marc at least go get Brando. She brought in two cups from the kitchen, one filled to the rim with instant coffee, the other with milk. Marc was sitting on the couch, reading some papers. She sat next to him, careful not to sit too close but acutely aware that all the distance in the world wouldn't be enough to keep her from wanting him.

"So what's the plan?" she asked, handing him the coffee.

"The plan?"

She reached for the papers he held. "Yes, the plan. You've been referring to this 'plan' of yours since you swung me over your shoulder." She looked at the top sheet and felt the blood drain from her face. It was the bulletin on Hooker's escape. Melanie had to scan it three times before she got the full scope of what the report said. Two days ago arrangements had been made to transport Hooker from the county jail to a holding cell at the courthouse. A guard had been escorting him from the cell to the courtroom when Hooker grabbed the guard's gun and made his escape.

But what caught her attention was a notation at the bottom of the page: Suspect believed to be seeking revenge against agent Melanie Weber.

Her hands shaking, she put her mug on the table then handed the papers to Marc, unable to read the report. She cleared her throat and looked to find him pointedly avoiding her gaze.

"Marc? You do have a plan, don't you?"

"You mean beyond keeping you safe?" He put his coffee cup on the table then sat back and stretched, but the coiled strength of his arm muscles revealed his true tension. "Nope."

Melanie stared at him. "You've got to be kidding?"

"Nope."

She glanced around the room, wincing at the bare bulb hanging from the ceiling fixture. "Let me get this straight. Hooker escapes from custody. You kidnap me. Take me first to your house, then haul me all the way out here to the coast of the Chesapeake—"

"Potomac."

She glared at him. "Okay, the Potomac. And now we're going to—"

"Wait."

"Wait for what? For Christmas?"

"If that's how long it takes for Hooker to be apprehended."

The weight of his words sank in. As did all the plans for her neatly mapped life. She moved her ring around her finger. "I can't just sit here for God knows how long waiting for Hooker to be picked up." Her voice dropped to a whisper. "I have things to do, Marc. Places to go..."

She realized what she'd said and looked at him. "I'm getting *married* the day after tomorrow."

"No, you're not."

She blinked very slowly. "What?"

He pushed up from his seemingly relaxed position and planted his well-toned forearms on his knees. "What I mean is that if Hooker is not caught between now and Saturday, you're not going anywhere near that church."

Why did she get the impression that's not what he meant at all? Could it be there was more behind the kidnapping than he was letting on? Was he merely taking advantage of the circumstances to stop her from marrying Craig?

But that didn't make a lick of sense. He'd had ample opportunity to seek her out before now. While she was in the hospital would have been a good time. After she found out she was pregnant would have been even better. But she hadn't received so much as a phone call from him. All this madness couldn't be about stopping her from marrying Craig.

Suddenly restless, she got up and started slowly pacing. "Tell me, Marc, why we're not going to do anything to help catch Hooker."

He immediately dropped his gaze, making his motives all the more suspect.

"You don't think I'm up for it, do you?" She moved to stand before him.

"Don't be ridiculous. You were my partner. You're just as capable as I am."

"Liar."

"I'm speaking the God-given truth." He reached for his coffee.

"Then why can't you meet my eyes when you say it?"

He looked at her, and she saw all she needed. She curled her fingers into her palms.

"You think that because I was shot, I'm some sort of invalid. Incapable of doing much more than sitting by idly while Hooker is caught."

His chuckle nearly knocked her off her feet. He took a sip out of the mug. He almost choked. "I don't think you're an invalid. Not exactly. Come on, Mel, I've been around others who have suffered injury in the line of duty, and it always takes a bit of time for them to get back up to snuff." He stared at the cup in his hands. "Milk?"

Melanie's face went hot as she realized he'd covered his cup with the report and had taken hers by mistake. She took her cup from him and put it on the table. "What makes you think I'm not? Up to snuff, I mean?"

"Seriously?"

She nodded patiently.

"Because if you were working at full tilt, you wouldn't be here right now. You would have laid me out the instant you saw me outside that damned rest room."

Melanie opened her mouth, but no sound came out. She clamped it shut. Slowly, her anger drained from her tired muscles, leaving her feeling suddenly vulnerable. He was right. At least partially. Of course, he had no way of knowing that her unresolved feelings for him had played a large role in her reluctance to fight him to her full capacity. And that just seeing him again had dealt a huge blow to her equilibrium.

Still, one well-placed blow to his solar plexus or his windpipe would have stopped him as effectively as any bullet. And she had done neither. Why? Up until now she had tried to convince herself she wasn't here of her own free will. What a crock that was. She'd been trained to stop professional assassins. Yet she had barely put up a token fight when Marc had thrown her over his shoulder and marched her out to his Jeep.

He cleared his throat. "Because if you were okay, you wouldn't have quit the division."

Melanie turned and paced, rubbing her forehead. She didn't know which was worse—having Marc think her incapacitated or having him know the real reason she had quit.

Still, spending the next unnumbered hours, days even, alone with Marc, doing nothing, was not an option.

"Maybe you're right," she said quietly. "But we could put some sort of plan together. You know, entrap Hooker."

His expression was dubious.

"Maybe this is just what I need. Something—a case—to sink my teeth into, you know, to oil my rusty skills."

He shook his head. "Nope. We stay here."

Renewed anger surged through her tense muscles. "And tell me, Marc, who died and made you all-knowing protector?" *No, no, no.* She wasn't going to get anywhere by arguing with him. *Think, Mel, think.* She continued pacing, carefully measuring her steps so as not to appear hysterical. "Okay. I admit I understand your initial motivation for kidnapping me. But we both agree that those aren't the circumstances now, right?"

"Uh-huh."

"Well, then, shouldn't we both have a say in what we should or shouldn't do?"

He turned his hands palms up, shrugged and sat back. "As long as it doesn't have anything to do with Hooker, sure."

Melanie bit her bottom lip to keep herself from swearing. "But isn't it in our best interest to make sure Hooker is apprehended as soon as possible?"

Marc laced his fingers behind his head, his expression growing decidedly playful. Mel fought not to watch the way his stomach muscles lengthened under the soft cotton of his shirt. "This is about that damned wedding again, isn't it?"

Melanie stared at him, wide-eyed. "This doesn't—I mean it isn't—"

"Admit it, Mel, everything was fine and dandy until I charged back into your life and messed things up."

It was suddenly impossible for her to swallow. "Don't you mean when Hooker escaped and restarted a nightmare I thought had ended?"

He rose from the couch in one long, languid move. "Nope. I mean when I charged back into your life."

"But you aren't back in my life, per se," she whispered. "We're no longer partners.…" She trailed off, watching as he moved ever closer. She fought to hold on to her words. "We're not partners anymore. Not in any sense of the word."

"And you want me to believe that in three months, you found someone who could replace what took us two years to build?" He was within breathing distance, and

Melanie did just that. She took in a long, slow breath, filling her senses with the utterly masculine smell of him.

Never one for expensive colognes, despite the many brands she bought for him for Valentine's Day, birthdays and Christmas, he preferred using a citrusy aftershave that enhanced rather than covered his unique smell. Obviously that hadn't changed. She fought the desire to hum, likening the smell to warm soap, lapping ocean waves and the pungent scent of a freshly peeled orange.

"I've known Craig for much longer than I've known you. A lifetime, in fact."

Marc reached out and caught a stray tendril of hair that had curled over her cheek. Suddenly incapable of drawing any breath at all, Mel merely watched him, shivering when he gently tucked the strand behind her ear. "Ah, yes, I remember you telling me about Craig. He was the one who lost his breakfast when you and he were assigned to dissect a frog in science class. Let's see if I can remember correctly. In the third grade, right?"

"Fifth," she said, her voice hoarse.

He met her gaze, the depths of his brown eyes dizzying. "Funny, Mel, I don't remember you telling me that you two had gone out."

"He was the first guy I ever kissed."

"On a dare."

This was not going well, at all. Yes, she knew she'd told him all this. She hadn't been aware he'd been listening. "There was always something between us...." Her gaze dropped to Marc's mouth, which was turned up in a teasingly suggestive smile. She licked her lips. "Between Craig and I, I mean." He didn't have to know it was friendship.

"Tell me something, Mel. Does he make you pant the way I did?"

The brush of his palm against her right nipple caused a massive shudder to travel the length of her body. She knew she should move away from him, protest the familiar, intimate touch, but she could do little more than stand transfixed, wanting him to touch her and…more.

"He makes me happy."

The smile finally vanished. "Outside of the bedroom. How's he going to make you feel inside?"

He cupped her breast, very obviously avoiding contact with the straining tip. She stifled a moan and tried to stop herself from leaning into his touch. "I'm sure he'll be very good."

"Oh? Has there been evidence of that?"

Another scrape of his thumb across her nipple, another shudder that seemed to begin and end in her heated core.

"I don't think this is a very good idea, Marc. We should, um—" she licked her lips again, her gaze fixed on his mouth "—we should be discussing how we're going to trap Hooker."

"Uh-uh." He slowly shook his head. "The only thing I'm interested in catching right now is you."

Despite all her arguments, she knew he already had her.

His mouth came down on hers. Mel gave up the fight and melted against him, surprised by how very much she had longed to feel Marc's arms around her. Only his arms weren't around her. His right hand still lay against her breast. His other arm was frustratingly at his side.

Melanie leaned closer, putting her arms around his neck and drawing him nearer, coaxing his tongue into her mouth, teasing him with little flicks of her own that she knew had once driven him crazy. Still he kept his free arm to himself.

Whimpering deep in her throat, she rubbed against him, pleased to feel his erection. Tilting her hips forward, she shimmied against him in a hungry way she knew not even he could deny.

And he didn't. Threading his fingers through the hair above her ears, he kissed her more thoroughly than he ever had, delving deeply into her mouth, his breath coming in rapid, telling gasps. Still, it wasn't enough for Melanie. She grabbed the back of his shirt, tugged it from the waist of his jeans, then plunged her hands under the soft material to touch the even softer length of his hot skin.

Before she was aware he had taken his hand from her hair, she felt his fingers graze the front of her damp panties. She nearly collapsed against him as a long shudder took hold of her, shimmering through her sex-starved body even as she moved her hips against his probing fingers. He groaned and slid his fingers inside the edging.

Oh, how long she had waited for this. Dreamed about this. Marc touching her…

"Yes, yes," she murmured against his mouth.

"No."

6

"NO," MARC SAID AGAIN.

It took a long, bracing moment to realize the word had come from his mouth. Beneath his fingers, Mel's skin was hot. Against his body, hers was soft and pliable. Against his mouth, hers was wet and seeking.

No? *No?* Why on God's green earth would he ever say no? He stared into her sleepy eyes and nearly groaned. He'd wanted to bury himself deep in her ever since he saw her coming out of that damn bridal shop. Hell, his need for her went back further than that. Way further. Back when he'd stood outside that damned hospital, battling demons he hadn't known still existed, holding that stupid ring. Demons that wouldn't allow him to set foot inside that cold, antiseptic building where people were supposed to heal. The only memories he had of hospitals were of people dying.

"No."

This time there was no mistaking the word had come from him. He was harder than steel, his blood pumped through his veins like an overworked locomotive, and Mel was hotter than she'd ever been for him. Even now her hungry mouth slid to his ear despite his words.

He grasped her arms and pushed her away from him. Her face was flushed and provocative, but despite the groan that echoed through him, Marc knew he was doing the right thing. Mel would hate him if he took advantage of her like this.

Take advantage of Mel. He nearly laughed out loud. If only his tortured body wasn't battling him for control.

Mel's drugged eyes searched his face. "Isn't this what you wanted, Marc? To make me pant at your feet?" He watched her swallow.

His fingers dug into her soft flesh. "Not like this. Not this way."

"What way, then?" She tugged her gaze away from his face and whispered, "This may be your last chance. In two days I become somebody else's wife." Was it him or had her voice cracked on that last word? "You might want to take what you can, while you can."

If any words were capable of proving he'd made the right decision about pulling away, those were. He refused to have sex with her while she was still determined to marry that—that Craig.

Good comeback, McCoy.

He forced himself to turn away from her, the action one of the hardest things he'd ever done. It fell a solid second. The first thing on the list was visiting Mel in that infernal hospital.

"I'm...I'm going to get the rest of the things out of the Jeep."

MELANIE STOOD near the barred window and rubbed her arms despite the heat as Marc moved around behind her, unpacking. Her body still pulsed with need. Her head swam with confusion. She couldn't guess at the reason he had pushed her away. Her ability to understand anything he did or felt was notably faulty.

Before their breakup, she had convinced herself he loved her. She'd thought she felt it in his touch when their lovemaking had become somehow more...meaningful. Slower, more thoughtful and ultimately more thrilling. Had thought she saw it in the depths of his eyes when he looked at her. Then the night before her run-in with Hooker, while lying slick and breathless in his arms, she had made the mistake of saying she loved him.

She closed her eyes against the memory. But it was useless. The lines of his shocked face were forever etched into her mind. She hugged herself to keep from remembering the way he'd practically leaped away from her. She'd found him so damned cute despite her pain that she'd nearly cried.

Then she'd been shot, and he had left her lying alone in the hospital.

Melanie tried to ignore the dull ache in her heart as she slowly turned to watch Marc disappear into the bathroom. She reminded herself that it hadn't been the only time she'd misread his intentions. She absently examined her wrists. She'd thought he'd thrown her over his shoulder earlier tonight to keep her from marrying Craig.

Her cheeks burned with the knowledge of how wrong she'd been…again.

She'd known from the beginning that Marc wasn't the type to commit. She even admitted that his aversion to commitment had proved a magnet of sorts. What woman could resist seducing a man of Marc's caliber into their way of thinking?

The room was unbearably quiet. She tried to find some relief in the idea that she'd chosen someone like Marc. A man with honor, dedicated to his career. A man who knew wrong from right. But did it really matter if she'd chosen him or a Johnny-Be-Bad Biker, when all was said and done? Ultimately she'd fallen in love with a man she couldn't have.

A man who would have as much interest in being a father as he'd had in being a husband.

She tightly closed her eyes, trying to quell the little thrills of awareness that continued to slink through her body. Despite the hunger for excitement that had propelled her to become a secret service agent and had ushered her into Marc's arms, ultimately she had wanted what every other woman wanted: love.

"Mel?"

She looked up at the sound of his voice. His concerned

expression made her put a hand to her face. She was crying...again.

Hating that her hormonally influenced emotions made her so weak, she scrubbed at her cheeks and whispered, "I must have some dust in my eyes."

He shifted, apparently uneasy. "Dust?"

She nodded, then lifted her chin. "Did you want something?"

He gestured toward the bathroom, where she could hear the water running. "Yeah, um, it's ready."

"Ready?" she repeated numbly, peering around him.

He seemed to hesitate, then moved aside. "Yeah, I thought, you know, maybe you would want to take a bath."

A bath? She blinked several times. Had he just said... No. He couldn't have. She hadn't taken a bath since... well, since forever. Both she and Marc were shower people. She looked into the bathroom and noticed the shower curtain had been tied back and that the showerhead was notably dry.

She also noticed that three dozen or so candles in varying colors and sizes had been lighted and placed around the small room.

Her gaze flew to Marc.

He was looking at the stupid fan. "I think I'll go fix us something to eat."

Eat? Melanie swallowed hard and watched as he hurried toward the kitchen, closing the door after himself.

For long moments, she stood firmly in place, staring first at the tendrils of steam rising off the filling tub, then the closed kitchen door. Finally, her brain began to work, however sluggishly, and she slowly entered the bathroom, closing the door behind her.

With the light from the flickering candles, the walls looked artfully worn rather than dingy. The illusion was helped along by the thick new towels folded neatly over the sink, the huge bath mat covering the floor and the nightgown hanging on the back of the door. She fingered the soft material, tears gathering in her eyes as she noted the high collar and the long length. Marc had always preferred her to wear lingerie that was a little more risqué, a little more transparent. That he had chosen this...

Her gaze trailed to the glossy pink bag she had spotted at the condo. It had been shoved into the wastebasket, one of the tags he must have cut dangling over the side. Everything before her indicated he *had* planned in advance. If only the overwhelming evidence didn't prove that this particular plan had nothing to do with protecting her from Tom Hooker.

She realized the water was about to overflow and moved to turn off the old-fashioned two-handled faucet. She trailed her fingers in the steaming water and breathed in the scent of— She picked up the bottle of bath oil. Her throat clogged. *Jasmine.*

She indulged in a watery smile. She didn't know what had gotten into Marc, but only he could do something so incredibly sweet at the most inappropriate time.

She stood up, not knowing quite what to do. Marc had not only carved out a safe haven for her by way of the cabin, he'd created an oasis of sorts, as well. She sat on the edge of the claw-footed tub and peeled off her panty hose, not sure what to make of his actions.

All she could think about was how heavenly the water smelled.

And how she should be careful not to read more into Marc's unusually thoughtful actions than was there.

MARC SET the last plate on the coffee table, then straightened, surveying his handiwork. The place didn't look so bad now that there were signs people inhabited it. He grimaced. At least he thought so. As for Mel...

His gaze trailed to the closed bathroom door. Left with nothing more to do until she came out, he stepped toward the door and listened. She'd been in there for a long time.

If there had been a window in there, he would have guessed she'd be long gone by now. But there wasn't.

He hadn't known how Mel would take the bath bit. He'd half-expected her to label him crazy, and he'd come close to pulling the plug himself. He'd found the idea in an article, "Ten Ways to Win Back Your Lover for Good." He'd thought the notion was a bit twisted, but he admitted finding the bath tempting once he'd filled the tub.

There was a sound. Quickly stepping back from the door, he wondered if the nervousness that charged through him was noticeable.

So far every point of his plan had gone horribly, terribly wrong. Rather than convincing Mel to drop her wedding plans and take up where they'd left off, he was sure he had further alienated her, though he wasn't exactly sure why. Which just wouldn't do at all.

The door finally opened, making him jump. So much for keeping his cool.

And so much for that nightgown he'd bought to keep his libido under control.

Uh-oh. Marc's gaze was plastered to Mel's uncertain expression. He tried to ignore the jutting of one curvy hip and the inviting way her breasts pressed against the pale silk that nearly matched the shade of her hair. He failed miserably.

"Hungry?" he asked, clearing his throat and flinching at his word choice. *Keep it safe, McCoy. Keep it simple. And keep it far away from anything to do with sex…for now.*

"Um, yes, a little."

Mel responded to his question, but she didn't move an inch from where she stood. She gave him one of those sinful little smiles of hers, shifted her weight from one bare foot to the other, then slid her hand down the length of the silk. Marc swallowed hard, watching the pale material mold to her perfect body.

He let rip a vehement curse and tore his gaze away from her.

It took every shred of control he had to ignore her. He noticed the slight quake of his hands, and his blood pulsed so thickly through his veins he could hear the roar of it in his ears. But he couldn't let happen what he was afraid was going to happen until he could prove to Mel he had changed. Maybe not in all the ways she wanted him to—*love* was a word that had never been used in the Mc-Coy household—but he did want her in his life, badly. Things had been good between them. So good. And they could be again.

And he was willing to do whatever it took to make sure that happened.

Mel finally moved, but the slinky way she did made him wish she had stayed where she was. With short, measured steps, she came to stand in front of him, the evidence of her arousal clearly evident by the two points smiling at him through the silk. His throat—along with another body part—tightened painfully.

"Shall I sit here?"

Before he could get a word out of his mouth, Mel turned to fluff the cushions on the couch. He'd always thought she'd had a great rear end, but the way the silk outlined the lush, rounded flesh...

It was then he realized there were no lines. *No lines.*

He'd forgotten to buy her panties.

I can handle this. I can handle this....

"Excuse me." His voice was barely a croak. "I'll be, um, right back."

He disappeared into the kitchen, switched on the broiler, then stood gripping the rim of the sink for dear life. He turned on the water and resisted the urge to plunge his head under the cold stream. Instead, he splashed his face several times.

He was afraid if he went back into the living room, he wouldn't be able to resist making love to her. And if he did that, he was sure he'd lose her forever. After Hooker was caught, she'd go away believing he'd only wanted her for sex. Which was what she'd accused him of before.

Nearly burning himself, he took the hefty helping of Cheddar fries and burgers from the broiler. Then he took a deep breath, praying for some major help to see him through this night.

He took the food into the living room and placed it on the table, along with the other things he'd set out. He'd made all her favorites. But as he watched her look it over, he thought she seemed about as hungry for food as he was.

He purposely knelt on the floor on the other side of the table, not about to test himself by sitting next to her.

"I...I bought some wine. Red. I know, um, how much you like red." At the time he'd thought it would help wash down the food if it hadn't turned out right. Now he realized how stupid the idea was.

His gaze was riveted on the outline of her soft, shapely breasts as he poured the ruby-colored liquid into two different-size tin cups. The wine spilled over his hand and splashed onto the coffee table.

"Mel..."

"I'll only have a sip or two." She avoided his gaze as she hesitantly took the smaller of the cups. "Yes?"

He watched her lips purse to sip, then her throat worked as she swallowed. Just beyond his vision, he saw her breasts sway against the nightgown. He kept his gaze glued to her face as she picked at a piece of green lettuce on her burger, then nibbled on it. A dollop of mayonnaise clung to her upper lip. Her too pink, too wet tongue dipped out to slowly lick it off.

Marc felt a groan grow deep in his chest. She didn't have a clue what she was doing to him. As far as she was concerned, she was merely sharing a meal with him. Nothing more. Nothing less.

He should have bought one of those granny gowns, and to hell with the heat.

No longer able to help himself, he allowed his gaze to travel south.

Talk, McCoy, talk.

As much as he hated to broach it, there was one subject that would throw cold water onto his libido, but quick.

He folded his paper napkin. "Do you love Craig?"

Marc cursed himself up one side and down the other. He had meant to discuss her relationship with Craig, but not in that direct way. He vigorously rubbed both hands over his face. But that particular unasked question had been haunting him all night. It was just as good it was out.

He chanced a look at Mel to find she had finally lifted her gaze to his. Her green eyes were dark in the candlelit room.

"I…" she said, then quietly cleared her throat, apparently struggling for an answer. "Yes, Marc. I do love Craig."

But not the way I love you, Melanie thought.

Melanie was half-afraid she'd said the second part aloud. But as she searched Marc's face, taking in his sexily disheveled brown hair, she knew she hadn't. And she would likely never tell Marc she loved him ever again.

"I see," he said, looking entirely too crestfallen.

She'd never known a man as irresistible as Marc. Even now, despite her hurtful confession. He'd taken off his T-shirt, apparently trying to beat the heat. The sight of his bare chest alone was enough to notch up her body temperature. She pulsed all over as her gaze followed the length of his hair-sprinkled chest—she longed to feel the crisp dark hair between her fingers—down to where his jeans hugged his well-toned waist.

She blinked and looked into his dark, shadowed eyes, longing for him to say something silly or make a wisecrack. Something, anything to break the growing tension, to slow the rapid beat of her heart. But he didn't.

She wasn't sure if it was the decadent feel of the silky nightgown against her clean skin or the sight of him looking so hurt and completely appealing, but she knew then exactly what she wanted. One more night with him. A few intimate hours to remember in the years to come. Quiet time before she told him she was pregnant. Before she married someone else.

She watched his gaze flick to her hands. She worried her engagement ring, then skimmed the clingy lines of the silk. But rather than avoid his gaze, as she had earlier, she sat up a little straighter, stretching her neck as a shiver started at the very tips of her toes and shimmied all the way up her spine. She felt, rather than saw, her nipples harden, and she opened her mouth to pull in more of the humid air. Marc might have failed Relationship 101, but she had plenty of proof that he had aced the course on body language.

Marc wasn't sure what had changed in Mel in the past few minutes, but he knew for a fact something had. He could tell by the way she sat up a little more provocatively, looking at him in that way that said so much. He'd never been able to refuse her. Never. It hadn't mattered where they were—in a restaurant, in the car—all she had to do was look at him that way, and he was all hers.

That hadn't changed.

Pure, primitive need filled him as he grabbed the edge of the table. He gave up trying to gain some leverage and instead tipped the table out of his way. The crash of tin, glass and plates was barely audible over his hammering heartbeat.

Threading his fingers through the hair above her ears, he suddenly stilled, holding her there, gazing deeply into her eyes. He needed to make sure this was what she truly wanted. If he saw a flicker of doubt…

Her hands encircled his wrists and slid up his arms, pulling him closer.

"Make love to me, Marc."

Her husky voice flowed over him like the silk that covered her lush body, chasing away any chance he had of pulling away from her. With a deep groan, he slanted his mouth across hers, tentatively at first, calling on every ounce of self-control at his disposal.

She tasted so sweet. Like a ripe pear begging to be eaten. Her tongue sought and found access to his mouth even as she slid closer to him, cradling him between her silk-clad thighs, pressing her breasts against his bare chest. He'd always thought that the closest he could come to heaven was through sex with Mel, but what he was feeling now, he couldn't begin to describe. It was like looking into the star-filled night sky, seeing all the answers to life's questions printed there and being unable to do anything more than admire them, bask in the peace they offered, but not being able to read them.

Tilting her head with one hand, he slid his other down the impossibly long column of her neck, feeling her pulse there. There was a sense of inevitability about this, their coming together now, tonight. As if he was no more in control of his actions than Mel was. His palm moved from the silk of her skin to the silk of her gown, finding very little difference except in the way the silk moved, gliding easily against her flesh as he cupped her breast.

She tugged her mouth away from his, gasping as she rested the side of her head against his. "You always knew just how to touch me," she rasped.

Her hands skimmed down his abdomen, causing him to catch his breath. She reached for and found the front of his jeans. Her knuckles grazed his skin as, one by one, she undid the metal buttons there, her mouth once again seeking his.

Marc drank deeply of her lips, groaning as she slid her hand inside his fly, freeing him and wrapping her silken fingers around his pulsing shaft. He nearly spilled his need into her palm right there and then. A part of his mind said it was because he'd gone so long without her. Another part told him what they were sharing was unlike anything they'd shared before.

Gliding the nightgown slowly up her long, long legs, he tried counting backward from a hundred, but lost track of the count when she flicked her tongue across his lips, then closed her mouth over his again.

Too soon. Too fast.

At the rate they were going, it was going to be over as soon as it had begun. He needed to gain some distance, and he needed to do it now.

Gently pressing her into the cushions, he ignored her needy protest, then grasped her hips and hauled her down so her rear end was even with the edge. Her lusty moan coaxing him on, he used his thumbs to part her and slowly bent to fasten his lips around the sensitive nub at her center.

Mel cried out and arched from the cushions, pressing herself against his mouth. He curved her legs around his neck, laving her with his tongue, reveling in her gasps and soul-deep moans.

She tunneled her hands through his hair, moving restlessly, both begging him to stop and pleading with him to give her the release she sought.

With his fingers, he spread her farther, running his mouth the length of her, licking, tasting her musky essence, then he slowly slid two of his fingers inside, readying her for him.

He knew her moment of crisis was near. Could tell by the way she almost desperately grasped the cushions, her hips going still. He fastened his mouth around her nub once more and gently sucked, holding on as she bucked from the couch in a series of uncontrollable spasms, contracting around the fingers he thrust into her slick wetness.

She looked at him through drugged eyes, her hair a tangled blond mass around her face, her lips parted provocatively.

He'd never wanted someone so much in his life.

Marc made quick work of taking off his jeans, his teeth

gritted so he would keep from climaxing before he claimed her the way he'd been longing to for the past three months. She sought and found his erection and led him home. As she surrounded him, he threw his head back. Damn her for making him want her this way. Bless her for showing him what it felt like to be alive again.

No…not yet…

But he couldn't wait. It seemed like forever since he'd been able to lose himself in Mel. Three torturously long months filled with wet dreams and cold showers, haunted by memories of her needy cries and soft sighs.

She rocked against him, pulling him in deeper, and he lost all concept of time and place as he thrust into her.

The instant he heard her cry out his name, he let loose, every muscle going rigid even as he tried to keep up the rhythm of his thrusts. But it was a losing battle. His hamstrings locked and his hips drove forward one last time, spilling his need deep inside her.

For long moments they stayed like that, joined together, connected in a way that somehow surpassed anything they'd shared before. Marc felt as if he was floating somewhere above his body, lighter than the heavy, humid air around them, curiously detached yet a part of every physical item in the room.

He reluctantly withdrew from her, then laid his head against her silk-covered stomach. He closed his eyes, unsure if it was his heartbeat he heard there, or hers.

MELANIE JOLTED AWAKE, her heart pounding in her ears, fear clogging her throat. Around her, the night was black and forbidding, the bed she lay in unfamiliar and hard. It took her a moment to realize where she was.

The safe house.

She'd dreamed. What? What had she dreamed? She desperately tried to hold on to the haunting images, to examine them, to understand why she had awakened and why she felt as if her heart was going to beat right through her chest.

Hooker.

In her mind's eye, she saw the shadowy figure somewhere twenty feet to her right near the first-floor window of the senator's house. The window was partially open, and the figure had been halfway in when she shouted. Then there'd been the flash of reflected light as Hooker had turned his weapon on her.

She closed her eyes and swallowed hard. The staff psychologist had told her the nightmares would lessen in frequency after a week or two. But here it was, three months later, and she still saw the vivid, haunting images almost nightly.

"Maybe the dreams are trying to tell you something," Judith Hamilton, the psychologist, had told her a couple of weeks ago.

"Yes, I think they are," Melanie had said. "They're telling me I did the right thing by quitting."

A low murmur brought Melanie's head around. Marc turned over and pulled her into his arms as naturally as if he'd been doing so forever.

For a long moment she stayed like that, trying to control her breathing, trying to enjoy the moment for all it was worth, all it signified—namely, the last time she and Marc would share a bed. But rather than wrapping herself in the warmth of his body, a bittersweet sadness gripped her from within. She burrowed against him, breathing in the smell of him, trying to ignore that he didn't have a clue what she had in mind.

After their frenzied lovemaking on the couch, they'd managed to salvage some of the food he'd prepared. She fed him the Cheddar fries, and he gave her bites of the salad with slow deliberation and languid care. The circumstances that had brought them together were taboo, and everything but the sound of the crickets had been off-limits. Melanie looked on their silence with the twenty-

twenty vision of hindsight. She supposed that since Marc couldn't say the things she had so longed to hear, there had been nothing to say.

But their bodies still had plenty to communicate.

Melanie swallowed past the emotion clogging her throat. She'd never felt so thoroughly made love to.

At least in her eyes they had made love. But she knew better than to make that mistake twice. In Marc's eyes…well, he'd likely see it as the best sex he'd ever had.

Dear, thickheaded, love-impaired Marc.

She dragged his hand to her mouth and kissed his fingers, loving the warm feel of his skin against hers. When he stirred, she gently moved his arm around her waist and held it there, wishing the baby within her could know the touch of his father. She tightly closed her eyes, clutching the memories from the night before, holing them away the way a squirrel gathered the biggest nuts to see him through the winter. Only the memories Melanie had gathered would have to last her a lifetime.

WHAT IN THE HELL was that infernal pounding?

Marc dragged the pillow over his head and groaned, groggily trying to remember how much he'd had to drink last night. There had been many times over the past weeks that he'd awakened, convinced someone was using a jackhammer just outside his window, only to find the curtains flapping against the frame.

Then he remembered he'd had very little to drink and bolted upright in bed.

Mel.

A quick, sweeping glance told him he was the only one in the room. The pounding was someone knocking at the front door.

The significance of that hit him in the gut like a sucker punch. He leaped from the bed, pulled on his jeans and rushed the door.

"Mel?" he called, nearly tripping over a confused Brando. "Sorry, buddy."

They were out in the middle of nowhere. It didn't bode well that Mel was nowhere to be seen and that someone was at the door. He picked up his empty gun holster, noticed his cell phone was missing and cursed. Quickly, he checked his jeans pocket. Relief washed through him. Good. The ring was still there.

Improvising, he grabbed the leg that had broken off the coffee table the night before. He yanked open the door, then brought the leg down.

"Whoa!" Connor ducked, lifting his arms to ward off the impending blow.

Cursing, Marc tossed the leg into the overgrown grass, then stared at his eldest brother. "Jesus, Connor, I could have maimed you for life." He dragged in a breath. "What in the hell are you doing here?"

A scowl marred his brother's face. "I think the better question would be what the hell are *you* doing here?" He tried to push through the door, but Marc stopped him. "Imagine my surprise when Pops wakes me up in the middle of the night to tell me the Maryland state authorities have been by asking around for you. Then this morning I'm putting my keys in my pocket when I notice a certain one missing. Damn it, Marc, do you have any idea what kind of trouble you could get us both into by breaking and entering into federal property?"

Marc scratched his head and looked past his brother. He was relieved to see his car was still there. That meant Mel had to be around somewhere. "I'm just borrowing the place for a couple days, that's all. I really wish I had the time to explain—"

"That's all? Have you lost your friggin' mind, Marc?"

Time or not, it was obvious Connor wanted an explanation and he wanted it now. But with Mel only God knew where, and with Hooker...

He took a long look at his brother. No one had known

where he was until now. Even one more person having that information doubled the risk of discovery.

Oh, God.

He grabbed Connor by his shirtfront. "Were you followed?"

"Let go of me right now, little brother, or else—"

"I asked if you were followed!" Marc said.

He abruptly released Connor then started to close the door.

Connor caught the barrier. How many times when they were kids had Marc pulled a fast one on his brothers only to have Connor following on his heels? And how many doors had Connor caught, preventing his escape?

"I'm not going anywhere until you explain this to me. Now. And why don't you start with what in the hell was going through that deranged mind of yours when you kidnapped Melanie Weber right under her mother's nose."

Marc ground his teeth together. "Later, Connor."

"Damn it, Ma—"

Needing to find Mel and not knowing how to get rid of his brother, Marc tried to push Connor out of the way just as Connor was taking a step forward. Connor stumbled, all his attention on grabbing the rickety iron railing. Marc quickly reached out to control his fall, then reached into Connor's suit jacket to slide his gun from his shoulder holster. He said, "Sorry about this, Con. I'll get the gun back to you later." He went inside and slammed the door. Connor dropped to the ground.

7

THE COOL SAND sucked at Melanie's high heels, making each step an impossible struggle. She hadn't realized that three months of inactivity would leave her so out of shape. At this rate, she'd only get twenty yards before Marc realized she was missing. He'd probably find her on her knees, gasping and wheezing and offering her soul up for a measly cup of coffee. Just one. It didn't matter that she hadn't had even a sip of the heavenly brew for nearly three months. She needed the caffeine jolt right now.

Marc had never been a morning person. That's one of the reasons it had been so easy to sneak out. Another was that after waking from that nightmare, she hadn't slept another wink. It had been all too easy to slip from the bed long before dawn to map out her escape.

Her heart gave a tender squeeze. Leaving Marc lying there alone had to be one of the more difficult things she'd ever done. He'd looked so boyishly handsome—almost vulnerable—and downright sexy. It was almost too easy to let herself believe everything would be okay. She'd tell him the truth about the baby and he'd...

She tripped over a piece of driftwood. He'd have a coronary—after he gave her the devil for keeping the information from him for so long.

Her thoughts focused on the exact reason she needed to get away from Marc, and fast. Yes, Hooker may be lurking out there somewhere, but the physical danger he presented paled in comparison to the romantic fantasies she was starting to entertain after a night of loving Marc.

Exasperated with the tears that threatened to flood her

eyes, Melanie set the heavy revolver in the sand and, still clutching the cell phone, took off the shoes Marc had brought in from the Jeep the night before. She looked between her torn dress and the revolver, then tossed the shoes into a nearby bush. She really hated to litter, but the shoes were the least important thing she had. And considering her impractical attire, there was no place for her to stick any of the items for safekeeping.

She picked up the firearm, making faster progress as she sprinted across the beach, barely aware of the sun rising to the east or the sounds of nearby gulls. When her gaze wasn't trained in front of her, it was darting behind her to the cabin that grew smaller and smaller as she ran.

Still no sign of movement. Relief and disappointment filled her. She was going to get away this time.

Stopping to catch her breath, she gauged the distance between her and an easily recognizable road. Not far. If she called her mother…

It occurred to her that Craig's name hadn't even emerged as a possibility. She tightly closed her eyes. Why was it that since yesterday, she seemed to look for ways to compare Craig to Marc? It wasn't as if she hadn't thought long and hard before accepting Craig's awkward proposal. She'd taken two weeks. Fourteen torturous days and sleepless nights alternating between crying and determining to put the pieces of her life back together.

Irritated with herself and her situation, she juggled the revolver and punched out her mother's phone number with her thumb.

Her mother picked up on the first ring. "Hello?"

"Mom?"

"Oh, good Lord, Melanie! Where are you? Are you all right? Is that—"

"Mom—"

"—madman still holding you hostage? I've been up all night worrying—"

"Mom!" Melanie's patience drained as she tried to edge a word in.

"—afraid he'd done something awful. You hear those stories in the news. Spurned lover kills his ex-girlfriend, chopping her into little pieces—"

Melanie tugged the phone away from her ear and stared at it. Chopping her into pieces? What was her mother watching?

"—they find her in some Dumpster in the back of a Chinese restaurant—"

"Mother! Listen! Are you listening to me? Look, if you don't be quiet for a minute... No, sorry, I really didn't mean to say be quiet—"

This conversation was worse than the sand that had nearly sucked off her shoes. Only with her mother, she'd be lucky to get out alive.

"And Craig! I nearly forgot about Craig. He's right here—"

"Mother—"

"Melanie? Melanie, is that you?"

Melanie instantly relaxed. "I'm fine, really I am, Craig. There's nothing to be concerned about." Craig would understand. Craig understood everything. She'd tell him where she was and he'd be here to pick her up.

"Melanie? This is your mother again."

Like she had to be told *that*. Her anxiety grew. At this rate Marc would find her in a heap on the sand bawling hysterically. She chanced a glance at the house. Her heart leaped into her throat. The back door was open.

She slapped her hand to her forehead, then lowered her voice. "Mother, look, I know you were worried about me... Listen to me! No, of course I'm not whispering. I need you to pick me up—"

Suddenly her words were cut off as a shot split the relative calm of the dawn landscape, sending gulls squawking toward the sky. A millisecond later a column of sand spat at her like a geyser, spraying the front of her dress.

Another shot followed, and the cell phone went flying from her fingers, her skin vibrating from the jarringly close call.

Oh, God.

Melanie hit the sand so hard it took her a full half minute to catch her breath. Those thirty seconds she used to scramble toward a nearby bush. Finally she was able to draw in air, and the raw, harsh sound stunned her.

Oh, God. Someone's shooting at me.

She looked toward the house. The door was still open, but Marc was nowhere in sight.

Then she spotted him. Crouched at the side of the cabin, he was barefoot and wearing nothing but that tight pair of jeans, a gun drawn as he scanned from his left to his right. Gun? She had his gun.

Another shot.

Melanie dove deeper into the brush.

She looked down to find her free hand covering her belly, an unconscious attempt to protect the life that grew there. Stinging tears flooded her eyes as the danger that had loomed around her like an intangible cloud for nearly twelve hours crystallized into stark, terrifying reality.

Wrapping her fingers around Marc's revolver, Melanie reached deep inside, seeking the stillness she had learned to count on to see her through on the job. Her heart thudded harder, and she choked back a tidal wave of panic. *Come on, come on.* Where once she had been able to count on herself, her talent for clear thinking, now it seemed every lick of knowledge had gone, leaving her feeling scared and vulnerable.

Think of the baby.

The harder she sought strength, the more panicked she grew. Then, suddenly, like a slow influx of cool air, stillness swept over her. It started in her chest and emanated outward, calming the tremor in her hands. She planted her feet firmly on the ground. She crouched, her breathing shallow but controlled, her sight swift and ears alert. *There.* The rising sun reflected off something dark and shiny near the road.

She quickly ducked and slipped the safety off the revolver. Hooker. It had to be him. Given the remoteness of the cabin, there was no way he could have accidentally found the place. He must have followed them from the inn or the town house. Not that it mattered. Right now, she was at a disadvantage. She knew approximately where he was, but he knew *exactly* where she was.

Forcing a swallow, she balanced the gun in both hands, the weight familiar and reassuring. She'd always been a crack shot. She prayed she hadn't lost her touch.

Another crack of gunfire. The bullet ripped through the bushes to her left. She sidestepped quickly, then revealed herself, aimed and squeezed off a round. The trigger had barely sprung back before she was under cover again and sprinting toward the house.

One yard, two yards…

Crack.

She dove into the sand headfirst, wincing at the mouthful of sand she took in. As soon as the round whizzed past, she was up, blindly shooting at her target, then running again.

"Mel, get down!"

She heard Marc's order, then fastened her gaze on him. He was nearer than she thought, and whatever sand remained in her mouth spewed out when he hit her head-on. He was shooting even as he fell on top of her.

The stillness she'd felt left her immediately upon coming in contact with his body. She didn't know if it was the fear that they might never be this close again, or if she was just awfully glad to see him, but she felt on fire, despite everything going on around them. The scent of gunpowder filled the air, and the sound of a car's tires squealing against asphalt ripped at her ears, but all she could think of was that she could feel the rapid beat of Marc's heart against hers. Irrationally, she thought, *That's just the way it should always be.*

She opened her eyes to find him looking at her. A quizzical glint darkened his eyes as he scanned her features. She realized she was about to pass out.

"You okay?"

She nodded, struggling to regain her wits. "Fine. I'm fine. Your cell phone's history, though."

His devilish grin made her smile. Her brain was on overload. One moment she was arguing with her mother on the phone, the next she was eating sand while an escaped criminal used her for target practice. That would make anyone a little loony, wouldn't it? But even as she tried to convince herself that's why she felt the way she did, her body told her something else. And growing evidence of Marc's arousal pressed into her thigh.

He rolled off her and leaped to his feet. "Get up, Mel." He offered his hand.

She took it. Standing, she took inventory of the new tears in the dress.

"Nice. Think we can market it?"

"Yeah, you can call it the hell-and-back look," she murmured.

Everything she'd been thinking, feeling, minutes before was gone.

"Well, if that wasn't a sign that we've overstayed our welcome, I don't know what is." Marc sighed.

She looked at him. "Hooker."

His gaze was intense. "You saw him?"

"No. But who else could it be?"

"You're right." His expression grew pensive. He paced a couple steps, then hopped when he stepped on something in the sand with his bare feet. She shivered as he turned to face her. "Out for a morning jog, were you, Mel?"

Recalling exactly why she had tried to make her escape, she sobered. She futilely tried to brush the sand from her dress as she headed toward the house. "Something like that."

He grasped her arm, pulling her to face him. "Why?"

Her throat growing tight, she handed him his gun. "You know why."

His gaze held her still. "Are you telling me that last night…"

His words trailed off, leaving her speechless. She stared at the sand beneath her feet and squinted against the brightness of the rising sun.

"That last night was about lowering my guard so you could take off?"

Looking at her feet, she ignored the squeezing of her heart and whispered, "If the shoe fits." She winced at the words, hating how callous they sounded. The last thing she wanted to do was hurt Marc. But he was making it very difficult for her to do anything else.

She cleared her throat. "Don't you think we should be getting out of here?"

"Why? So you can just dump me at the first opportunity?"

She eyed him thoroughly. She didn't like what she'd said or the impact it had on him. But if it helped put her on equal footing, then that was what was important. Wasn't it?

One thing the last ten minutes had made painfully clear was that going home, returning to the neat little plans she'd made, wasn't an option. But she hoped where she went from here was.

"I promise not to ditch you if you agree to being partners on this," she said, pushing the words through her tight throat.

"Come on, Mel—"

Her heart beat an even, powerful rhythm, giving Melanie an important element of her life she'd lost months ago. *Control.* A sure sign was the echo of her mother's voice in the back of her mind telling her there were some things a woman wasn't meant to do. Couldn't do. Things the past few months had made Melanie believe she no longer should do. But right now, right this minute, her survival instinct kicked in pure and strong. She needed to protect not only herself, but her baby. And to do that, she needed to be in control of the situation. If not as leader, at least as partner.

"Marc, please listen to me. If what happened proves anything, it's that I am far from safe just sitting still waiting for the proper authorities to pick up Hooker. I'm going to have to track him as deliberately as he's tracking me." She cleared her throat, the reality of the words chilling her. "Either you're in or you're out. It's your call." She tried for a shrug as nonchalant as any he'd ever given her. "Makes no difference to me."

Suddenly, he grinned. Not a "You're killing me, Mel," grin, but a grin that said something more. She felt her face grow hot. Instead of turning away, she met his gaze.

"Now that's more like the Mel I remember." He handed her the gun. "So are you ready to go hunting, partner?"

MARC DIDN'T KNOW what to believe. He was acting more on instinct than wisdom. Why had Mel run? He watched her curvy little behind, clad once again in the pink dress, as she opened the door to a posh D.C. hotel room. He groaned. He didn't want to feel anything more than professional respect for her. Not any more. If she could leave him after last night…

Despite the partnership deal they'd struck, he was having trouble indulging in conversation with the new, reanimated Mel. On their ride to the city, she'd broached nearly every subject. Correction—every subject that had anything to do with Hooker. Sharing with Marc the details of the first letters Hooker had written—she'd sent the rest back unopened—telling him the frequency of Hooker's phone calls where he professed his innocence.

And of course she'd grilled Marc on everything he'd picked up over the past few weeks.

Throughout much of it, he'd remained silent, his hands attached to the steering wheel until he realized he was trying to pulverize it in his grip. All he could think of was he needed some space to think. Considering he'd had far too much space in the past three months, and that he'd been trying to get her to talk since he'd first put her into the back of his Jeep the day before, his reaction was not only unexpected, it was aggravating.

He rubbed the back of his neck. He felt used. Violated. Cheap.

He grimaced. He was reading too many of those damned magazines.

"We should be at some fleabag motel on the outskirts of town instead of in a four-star hotel," he said under his breath, holding open the door so she could maneuver herself and the shopping bags she carried inside.

"What makes a motel safer?"

He glanced around the long fifth-floor hall, scoping out the fire exit directly across from their room. "Escape routes."

She set the bags on a puffy, flowery ottoman and began rifling through them. "We've stood post at this hotel countless times. We both know exactly where the escape routes are, so what difference does it make?" She took a bra and a pair of panties from one bag, then a pair of jeans from another. "Besides, after where we stayed last night, I could do with a soft bed, cable and a bit of comfort."

Comfort? He felt as though he was soiling the room just being in it. And every negative comment she made about last night jabbed at him like a well-placed punch.

He put down the pet carrier and his bag.

He turned to find her emptying a small amount of kitty litter into a box. He pulled a can of cat food from his bag—the contents of which he purchased when Mel was buying clothes. He let Brando out, holding the can up when the overgrown tom wound around his ankles. "Well, you're none the worse for wear. You probably slept through the whole thing, didn't you, sport?"

He looked up to find Mel watching him in a way he couldn't immediately identify, a way he didn't particularly welcome. Her face had gone all soft while her eyes held a faraway look. "What?" he grumbled, shifting uneasily.

Her cheeks reddened, and she immediately dropped her gaze. "Um, I'm going to go take a quick shower, you know, before we get down to work." She glanced toward the bathroom door. "Why don't you order up some room service? Brando's not the only one who's hungry."

He opened the can, then put it on a bag on the floor. Brando swooped down on it like a ravenous fiend, making a rumbling sound between a growl and a purr as he knocked the smelly stuff back.

Despite the little they'd eaten in the past eighteen hours, food didn't appeal to Marc at all. But talking to room service personnel would give him something to do while he waited for Mel. And it would get his mind off trying to figure out exactly what he was feeling and why.

He hesitated when it came to ordering for Mel. Last night he'd fixed all her favorites, and she had eaten the salad and lettuce and tomato off both their burgers. When the room service lady got impatient with him, he made up his mind and ordered her a salad and a burger and fries for himself.

He slowly hung up the receiver and found himself right back to square one.

Sitting on the bed, he listened as Mel turned on the shower, and the restlessness within him grew larger than life. He realized that a lot of his agitation had to do with the fact that he'd been unable to protect her—again. She could have easily been hit, or worse, this morning. He shoved his fingers through his hair. Between when he figured out what was going on and when he tackled her to the sand, he'd known a fear unlike anything he'd ever experienced. It had paralyzed him. Made him focus on protecting Mel and Mel alone when he'd known the best way he could protect her was by incapacitating Hooker.

Instead, Hooker had gotten away and lived to shoot at her another day.

The new direction of his thoughts wasn't any more comforting than the last. Snatching up the receiver again, he put in a call to Connor at work. By now his brother should have recovered from the fall he'd taken, and his anger should have lowered to a slow simmer. At least that's what Marc was banking on because he had a few favors to ask.

"McCoy," his older brother answered.

"Connor, hey, it's Marc...."

After a good talking down and a promise for revenge, Marc found out Connor had been on the property when the sniper hit. He'd followed the plain black sedan with no plates but had lost the perp shortly thereafter. He'd returned to the cabin, but Marc and Mel had already gone. He also learned that no new word had been posted on Hooker's whereabouts. Connor promised to call if he found out anything, official or otherwise.

Marc hung up the phone, frustrated to still hear the sound of the shower. At this rate, the woman was going to wash herself down the drain.

He sprung from the bed and vigorously rubbed the back of his neck. Yes, he always experienced a certain charged tension after a close call, but this... His muscles were coiled so tight he expected them to pop at any second. His mind kept fastening on the image of Mel's wet, soapy body in that shower just a few feet and a wall away. *Damn.* Why had she run that morning?

He strode across the room and retrieved his bag from the top of the television. *The Feminine Mystique* was written across the glossy cover of the magazine he slid out. Glancing toward the bathroom where the shower was still running, he opened to the table of contents and found the page of the article. God, if Mel—much less any of his brothers—caught him reading this stuff…

He grudgingly admitted that he didn't believe Mel when she implied she used sex to distract him the night before. No woman could be that good at pretending. But why would she tell him that? It didn't make any sense. It could be, as the magazine suggested, she needed to keep a part of herself to herself. He wondered how much else Mel was keeping from him.

More than likely, her hurtful—God, where had he gotten *that* word?—remark was because she was afraid all her new, well-laid plans would get mussed up by their taking up where they left off.

He groaned. Only they hadn't taken up where they left off, had they? He stuffed the useless magazine under others on the phone table and started pacing. He was starting to relate on a personal level to the magazine pieces, which was not part of the plan at all. Why didn't men have a periodical that could help them understand what was going on with the opposite sex? Oh, yeah, he'd read that book that said men and women were from different planets, not once, but twice. Not that it mattered. He could read it a hundred times and still never really get what the guy was saying. Besides, he couldn't seem to budge the image of himself as an Invader From Mars alien every time he thought about it.

He picked up his pacing. Something about his feelings for Mel, his reaction to her, had changed since he'd carted her away the night before. He couldn't quite put his finger on what, but he knew they were more intense, vivid.

Then there was the sex.

God, he got rock hard just thinking about the way she had moved beneath him, over him, how it had felt to have her slick muscles surrounding him again. Things had always been great between them in bed, but last night…

This was getting him absolutely nowhere. He needed a

safe distance between him and Mel. He needed to stay alert, keep his eye on the ball and catch Hooker before Hooker had another chance to squeeze off a round at Mel.

And he needed to keep away from all those damned magazines.

MELANIE LEANED against the wall, her breasts unbearably sensitive, her body pulsating with the rhythm of the water. Where was he?

She knew it was crazy, masochistic even, to want Marc again after the morning's events, but she was coming to accept that life didn't make much sense. How could she want a man so badly with her heart and body, and know with her head he was all wrong for her? How could she run away from him, knowing it was the right thing to do, then try to tempt him into making love with her again?

She knew finding Hooker should be top priority right now. But she also knew that when he was found, there would be no excuses left to be with Marc. And that understanding opened up a whole new ache in her heart and made her want to take as much as she could while she could.

Peeking through the half-open shower curtain, she saw no sign of Marc. How long was she going to have to stay in here waiting for him?

She swallowed hard. She had lobbed quite a blow at his ego on the beach when she'd suggested their lovemaking had been nothing but a way to freedom. She closed her eyes and leaned her forehead against the tiled wall. What had she been thinking? She *hadn't* been thinking. At least not all the way through to the end. All she'd known at that moment was that Marc had charged back into her life and turned everything upside down. And she was having a hard time accepting that.

And that was saying nothing of his new attitude toward her. He acted as if she hadn't gone through the exact training he had, covered the same assignments, protected the same subjects. Suddenly, to him, she was this helpless little thing who needed taking care of. Needed someone to take the load from her fragile little shoulders. A big, strong man to make all the bad things in the world go away.

She moved her face into the spray. Marc was going to have to get it through his thick head that she could take care of herself, thank you very much.

An image of the sniper flashed through her mind, and she groaned.

Okay, so maybe she had lost her touch since taking that shot three months ago. Maybe the wound and the resulting shake-up of her life had undermined her confidence, clouded her thinking. She slowly ran the bar of soap over her belly, reflecting on all the changes that had resulted from that one moment. Fear itself was healthy, necessary, as long as she had some control over it. It was when she lost that control that things became dangerous.

It had been fear that had paralyzed her and fear that had shown her the way to the stillness she had lost what seemed like a lifetime ago.

The spray continued to pound. She peeked through the open bathroom door. At this rate, she was going to turn into a prune before Marc figured out what she was up to. She clutched the melting soap and began lathering herself all over again from the neck down.

Come on, Marc.

Last night…

She swallowed hard. Their time apart may have played a small role in the heightening of emotions, but last night there had been something more, a sensual intensity, an acute liberation in their coming together.

She tried to remember what it was like at the beginning of their relationship. Before she heaped so many expectations on top of it. But even then, there had been a shadow of hesitation, a list of reasons why they shouldn't be doing what they were. She supposed it stemmed from the fact that they worked together. Even the first time was supposed to have been their last. An accident, Marc had said. Yes, an unfortunate turn of events, she agreed.

Then came the second and the third times, and the excuses lost their edge until they stopped making them at all.

Melanie sank her teeth into the flesh of her lower lip, thinking that would have been about the time she started falling in love with him.

And what about all her plans? She had believed herself independent, liberated, and now she was mapping out a traditional route as if her life were a road impervious to earthquakes, floods and all forms of natural disasters.

Then came Hurricane Marc.

She looked down to find her hands resting over her stomach as if protecting the growing life within.

An image of a little boy emerged in her mind. A little boy who had her light hair and Marc's large brown eyes. A child who would have all her practical traits, yet would face life with the same zeal his father did.

Following closely on the heels of that image was one of her mother. She was probably climbing the walls. But not the walls of her house. She'd likely be camped out at the local sheriff's office, directing activities. From the minute, making sure fresh coffee kept running, to the elaborate, ordering deputies to comb the countryside for her.

The thought might have made her grimace before, but Melanie found herself smiling. There were a lot of unresolved issues between her and her mother. But ever since she learned she was pregnant, her perception of her mom had shifted. Wilhemenia had spent more than half her life obsessing over her two daughters, fighting to keep their house, working to keep Melanie and Joanie in tennis shoes. She had sacrificed her life for the sake of her children after the death of her husband. No, she had never remarried. No, Melanie couldn't recall her mother ever going out on a date. Not even after she and Joanie had left the nest.

She understood her mother better now. She felt the same fierce need to do everything it took to protect and provide a loving environment for the baby growing within her. Even if it meant sacrificing her needs to do so.

"Mel?"

Startled, she instinctively reached for the shower curtain to cover herself. Which went against her decadent plans.

She opened the curtain. Marc stood in the bathroom doorway, looking at everything in the elegant little space besides her.

He cleared his throat. "You planning on using all the water in the hotel?"

She wanted to shake him. Instead she pushed the curtain open even farther.

"Jesus, Mel, you're getting the floor all wet."

Without looking at her, he yanked the curtain almost all the way closed.

She grabbed his hand with her wet one. Finally his gaze moved to her face.

"You know, McCoy, sometimes you can be as thick as shag carpeting."

His eyes narrowed. "Thick, huh? No, I think thick would be me climbing into that shower with you." He craned his neck, obviously struggling not to look at anything but her face. "Look, you want to go, the door's right there. You don't have to sleep with me to escape."

Melanie opened the curtain and slipped her wet fingers along his jaw and into his dark hair. "I don't want to go anywhere, Marc. Not right now."

"Come on. You're getting me all wet."

Melanie smiled. "That's the whole point."

Finally, a reaction. A flick of a gaze to where the water sloshed over her breasts. Melanie swallowed hard. *Yes.*

"No." Marc grasped her wrists and tugged her hands from his face. "Room service will be here any minute."

Forget room service. Melanie fought to hold on to her smile.

His gaze dipped a little lower. A languid shudder ran through her. He hesitantly lifted his fingers, and she stopped her movements, realizing he was looking at her scar.

Last night it had been too dark for any visual exploration. And while the physical reminder of what she had gone through had been a constant presence for her, Marc had never seen it.

She swallowed hard as he gently ran the tip of his index finger across the pink, puckered skin. Then his eyes met hers.

Before she knew it, she was in his arms, her slick, soapy body against his clothed one.

8

MARC LANGUIDLY TRAILED a finger across Mel's belly, lightly touching the damp tangle of hair between her thighs. He grinned at her quick intake of breath.

"Again?" she rasped.

His chuckle shook the bed. "I don't think so." He gently tugged on her hair, earning him a laughing shriek. "I need at least a week to recover after today."

Her sudden stillness tipped him off to the change in her demeanor. He dragged his head from where it lay against her breasts and glanced at her face.

Sure enough, the light had drained from her green eyes, and when she sighed, it was as if she bore the weight of the world on her stomach instead of just him.

"What's the matter?" he asked, running a fingertip over the scar that represented so much in their relationship.

"Nothing."

Nothing? "Hey, that's my line."

She finally looked at him rather than through him. Then he realized what had precipitated the change in her mood. He'd mentioned time. *I need at least a week to recover....*

She reached for a towel that lay nearby, and Marc let her up so she could wrap it around herself. He wanted to protest the covering of her delectable flesh, but bit the impulse back. He might not know what was going on in her head, but he knew the meaning behind her physical movements. He wouldn't have a week to recover for another bout.

He rolled onto his back and draped his arm across his forehead. He couldn't imagine his life without Mel in it. While he was sure he and Mel had gotten physically closer, he also felt an emotional rift no amount of advice could help him bridge.

And it hurt like hell.

He rubbed his hands over his face. "I never thought I'd hear myself say this, but I almost hope you get pregnant."

She jumped off the bed so quickly, the movement of the mattress nearly catapulted him off the other side.

"What?" Her voice was a hoarse rasp.

Despite the tightness in his chest, he was amused by the way she clutched the towel—as if he already hadn't tasted everything that lay beneath it.

He shrugged. "Have you noticed we didn't use any protection?"

She remained mute, staring at him unblinkingly.

He cleared his throat, not entirely sure he liked her reaction. Was she so averse to the thought of having his child? "You know, we didn't use a raincoat, a rubber, a cond—"

"I know what protection means, Marc." He grimaced, watching her hands shake as she tucked in the towel.

He sat on the bed and reached for his briefs. "You don't have to act like I just suggested you become a live organ donor, for God's sake."

She started shaking her head in an odd way. "No, no, it's not that. I…" Her hand went to her throat as if trying to work the words out. "I want to know what you meant when you said you wished that I was pregnant."

It was his turn for the words to get caught. And boy, did they. To make matters worse, they seemed to have claws, and clutched at his throat for dear life. "I said I *almost* wish. Big difference."

Uh-oh. The homicidal look on her face explained why he'd had difficulty saying the words. Unconsciously he knew they would get him into a heap of trouble. And he knew Mel wasn't reaching for that pillow because she was tired. Although Lord knew she should—

She hurled it at him.

He caught it easily, and she made a sound of frustration. Dropping the pillow, he raced across the mattress and grabbed her, pulling her onto the sheets even as she clutched the bedside lamp in both hands.

"Give me that."

She struggled against him. "Let me go!"

He was glad her towel had come loose and circled her legs, pinning them—it kept her from causing any major damage.

"Give me the lamp, Mel." She sank her teeth into his shoulder. "Ow! Would you stop that!"

He pried the lamp from her fingers and dropped it to the floor. It shattered, despite the plush carpeting. He cringed, wondering how much that little knickknack was going to cost.

"What is it with you?" he asked, catching her chin, preventing her from taking a hunk of flesh from his shoulder. He searched her face. He'd never seen her this worked up. "Is it because I said I *almost* wished you were pregnant?"

Her answer came by way of a kick to the shin.

"Geez, Mel, would you tell me what in the hell is going on?"

The towel was coming loose.

"Come on, we talked about this a long time ago. Even before we started sleep—er, dating. I told you I didn't want kids."

She went suddenly still. He didn't dare move his hand, though. Not until he was sure this wasn't a diversionary tactic.

"Besides, aren't you the one who's marrying somebody else tomorrow?"

Aw, shit. Were those tears in her eyes?

He finally let her go and quickly moved to the other side of the bed. "What is it with you, anyway?" He ran his hands through his hair, his blood surging through his veins. He could handle almost anything from her. Silence. Her penchant for whacking him in the arm. Her sexy seductions. But her tears—he couldn't handle those.

The first time he'd seen them had cut him to the bone. The night Hooker shot her. She had gritted her teeth and paid close attention until she was sure Hooker was in custody, but the instant she looked down, her voice had cracked.

"*So much blood.*"

Marc had stared at her, unsure who had said the words, her or him. It had been all over, the blood. So much, he wasn't sure exactly where she'd been shot or how many times. Then Mel had started crying. *Crying.* That more than anything had scared the hell out of him. Mel wasn't a crier. She was one of the guys. She was supposed to be telling crude jokes, keeping a stiff upper lip and all that.

He leaned his forehead against his hands. That night had driven home how very different they were.

"I don't get you, Mel." He pressed his thumbs against his eyelids to block the images. "Three months ago you just break things off. No explanation, no goodbye, no I hope it was good for you, too. Then the next thing I hear you're marrying somebody else."

She rounded the bed and stood in front of him. "Do you really want to get me, Marc? Do you want to know the real reason I quit the division?"

He narrowed his eyes, trying to ignore that she was still naked. Trying harder still to ignore his instant arousal. "Yes."

She picked up the pillow he'd dropped. She whacked him a good one. "I am pregnant."

Marc sat ramrod straight on the side of the bed, dumbfounded, the pain from her hit not stinging nearly as much as her words. "What?" His voice was a croak.

She lifted the pillow again, then dropped it and sank

onto the mattress beside him. She whispered, "I said I am pregnant, you twit."

Since she was no longer directly in front of him, he stared at the window. A strange tingling began at the base of his skull, then inched over his head, chasing out every chaotic thought, every coherent word. "When? How?"

Out of the corner of his eye, he saw her press the pillow to her belly. "You *really* don't want me to answer that, do you?"

He imagined he could hear the creak of his neck as he turned to look at her. Her eyes were squeezed shut, and she clutched the pillow so tightly he expected it to split open and cover them both with feathers. "Either Craig is a very fast worker—"

She sprang from the bed, but before she could whack him upside the head with the pillow again, he grabbed her wrists, holding her still.

"Would you just hold on for a minute? You didn't let me finish." He strengthened his grip. Not because she still needed to be restrained, but because he needed the connection to ground himself. "What I was going to say is— and don't you dare hit me again or I swear to God I'll tie you to the bed—either Craig is a very fast worker, or I'm..." The thought of tying her to the bed was preferable to the words he couldn't seem to push from his throat. "Or I'm—"

"Going to be a father," Mel finished softly for him.

Marc felt as though he'd been caught on the wrong end of Mike Tyson's left hook. He worked his mouth around some kind of agreement, but no words came out. He could only stare at her. His gaze lingered on her face, dropped to her still bare, still wonderfully, deceptively flat stomach, then to her face again.

Then odd details combined to make a supportive whole. The urgency of her wedding plans. The fact that she drank milk rather than coffee. Her quitting the division to become a security consultant.

She nodded slowly.

"Well." He thought the word had come from his mouth, but he wasn't entirely sure. It sounded too high-pitched, too contrite to have possibly been his voice. But since he was watching her mouth, and nothing had come out of there, then—

"You're hurting me, Marc."

He winced and quickly released her wrists, watching as she rubbed them.

"Sorry," he mumbled.

She stepped quickly away from him and put on one of the hotel robes. She looked crazily small and delicate in all that thick, white terry cloth. "For what, Marc?" She knotted the belt and swiveled to face him. "Are you sorry about running out on me three months ago?"

Running out on her? Who ran out on her?

"Are you sorry for kidnapping me yesterday?"

Kidnapping her? He thought they'd moved past that.

"Oh, no, wait, I know what you're sorry for. You're sorry I'm pregnant." Her voice cracked. "Aren't you?"

He opened his mouth, then snapped it shut again.

Her gaze dropped to the floor. "Too late," she whispered. "I'm well past the twelve-week mark, so abortion is out. Not that I'd have one, mind you. I found out I was pregnant when I was in the hospital. Alone. With no one but my mother and sister around to prove that someone *did* care about me."

"I didn't mean—"

"Didn't mean what, Marc?" She seemed to shrink into the depths of the robe. "Tell me."

Yes, Marc, spit it out, man. He silently cursed himself. "I meant I'm sorry for hurting you. Your wrists, I mean."

She looked at the ceiling and gave an exasperated groan that made him cringe. He'd said the wrong thing. Again.

Why was it he could never say the right thing to her?

No matter what his response, it never failed to send her straight over the edge.

"What?" he asked, growing irritated. "What did you expect me to do when you sprung the news on me, Mel?" He grabbed his jeans, putting them on without his briefs and giving up on buttoning them after several failed attempts. He stalked toward her. "Or *were* you planning on telling me?"

A SHOCK OF PANIC shot through Melanie. She had expected anger from Marc. Had even planned for his dumbfounded expression when she blurted the news. What she hadn't predicted was the formidable, sober man facing her.

She turned and tugged on her panties under the privacy of her robe. Her cheeks burned, her heart thudded, and even she knew her dressing was a way to buy more time. She gave Marc credit when he didn't interrupt. He stood silently while she put on the jeans and the tank top she had bought.

"Of course I planned to tell you," she said softly, not daring to meet his gaze as she draped the robe over a chair back.

"When, Mel? When were you planning to tell me?" His voice was low.

She shivered, then bought a little more time by putting a sheer white blouse over the teal blue tank. She made a ceremony out of tying it at the waist. When? Good question. She really hadn't known when she was going to tell him. That had always loomed somewhere out on the horizon. The only thing she had been sure about was that she *would* tell him.

Then came yesterday, and the kidnapping, moving the time scale up so fast she got dizzy just thinking about it.

What a difference a day makes.

Marc took a step closer to her. Her gaze was riveted to his stony face. "When, Mel? After you got married?"

She didn't answer. She was too surprised by the myriad emotions plainly visible on his handsome, unshaven face.

While he was obviously hungry for an answer, she also noted pain lurking in the depths of his eyes. Before yesterday she had never seen him so serious, so direct. Suffice it to say she would never have used those two words to describe Marc McCoy at any point in their relationship.

He crossed his arms, emphasizing the clean lines of his forearms. "Well, seeing as your wedding is only a day away, I think it's safe to say you were planning to tell me *after* the nuptials." His eyes narrowed. "Although I'm not convinced you planned to tell me at all."

"Of course I was going to tell you. I told you now, didn't I?"

"Only under duress."

Duress? Yes, she would describe what she was feeling as duress.

You deserve every harsh lash he can dole out, her subconscious taunted.

God, how bad was it when her own subconscious berated her?

Very bad. Awful.

"Look, Marc, I…" Her heart contracted. "I did plan to tell you. You'll have to trust me on that." She anxiously brushed her hair from her face. "I do have to admit I don't really know *when* I would have done it."

He stood, a tall and silent sentinel, waiting for her to finish. Problem was, she was done. That's all she had to say. She had thought in vague terms. She envisioned Marc playing a role in their child's life. Long weekends, some holidays, things of that nature. Even though merely imagining him standing on her doorstep on a weekly basis and not being able to touch him turned her inside out. But that all had depended on her telling him he was going to have a child.

"Does…he know?" Marc shifted, appearing uncomfortable. "Craig?"

It was the first time he had said her fiancé's name in an uninsulting tone, which alerted Melanie to the seriousness of the question. And warned of the consequences should she tell him the truth. But if her current situation proved anything, it was that putting something off didn't avoid the hurt. It only made things worse.

She closed her eyes. "Yes," she breathed.

He didn't curse. Didn't yell at her. He didn't even blink. He nodded once, as if understanding something she couldn't quite decipher.

Melanie hurried about the room, burning off the nervous energy filling her. After she had collected discarded towels, placed all the dishes on the service cart, wheeled it into the hall and stuffed her ruined dress into the shopping bag, she turned to find Marc hadn't moved.

Her heart surged into her throat, choking off her air supply, filling her eyes with tears.

"Marc?"

He didn't respond, just stared at the spot where she'd been standing earlier.

"I'm sorry," she whispered.

She stood with her hands fisted at her sides, willing herself not to turn away. In all the scenarios she'd envisioned when she told him she was pregnant, she never thought she'd be the one apologizing. Until this very moment, she'd adamantly believed she was the one who deserved the apology.

Now she realized she'd punished him for crimes he hadn't committed.

I was alone and pregnant.

He didn't know she was pregnant.

He won't make a good father.

She'd never thought she'd make a very good mother until the choice was taken away from her.

He's going to run in the other direction when he hears this one.

He hadn't.

He finally moved. She jumped without knowing why. The suddenness, maybe. The fact that he had moved at all.

"Tell me, Mel, how does this, my knowing, impact your plans?"

Everything that had happened in the past three months slipped through her mind. The hospital. The doctor's shocking news. Marc's unexplained absence. Craig's proposal of marriage.

"I honestly don't know." And she didn't. After all that had passed between Marc and her, she couldn't see herself marrying anyone else. Not even Craig.

He blinked once, slowly. Then he moved again. He finished dressing and came to stand in front of her.

"I know what you're going to do. You're getting married tomorrow," he said, his gaze lazily traveling the length of her body and lingering on her stomach. "But it's going to be *me* you're marrying."

9

MELANIE STARED at the passing countryside with no concept of where they were or where they were going.

After Marc's staggering pronouncement, he'd hustled her out of the hotel via the back entrance and deposited her in the Jeep. She was aware of little more than taking the pet carrier he'd given her before leaving the room.

What had he meant by saying she was going to be getting married tomorrow to *him*? The mere thought was enough to start her heart racing. Swallowing, she vaguely registered that they were still in the city. Was he taking her to the town house? She looked in his direction to find him almost relaxed. As if their recent conversation hadn't taken place.

She watched a woman, stranded at the side of the highway, fixing a flat tire. It struck her that she once thought that would be one of the worst things to have happen, to be stuck out in the middle of nowhere. Now she knew better. But she also knew enough to know that no matter what the situation, things could always get worse. Her heart gave a triple beat. Or better.

She shifted in her seat to face Marc, her knee brushing his thigh. "What did you mean back there?"

"Back where?" he asked a little too innocently.

She kept her gaze steady.

He shrugged. "I meant exactly what I said."

She gestured nervously. "Which is?"

"Are you losing your hearing along with the good sense God gave you?" He grinned from ear to handsome ear.

Melanie barked with laughter, surprising herself.

She tried to school her expression into one more befitting the situation.

He'd told her once about his father's fatherisms. "With the good sense God gave you" was a popular one. That he'd used it to lighten the mood gave her hope. Hope that this was nowhere as serious as she'd feared.

She bit her bottom lip, unable to completely wipe the lingering smile from her mouth. "So let me get this straight. Tomorrow," she said, drawing the word out and indicating a point on her jeans with her finger, "I'm getting married."

"Uh-huh." He flicked on the blinker and exited the highway. Moving away from the city, she noticed distantly, as he continued west on a two-lane state route.

"But I won't be marrying Craig."

He nodded as if indulging a particularly slow child. "Uh-huh."

Her smile widened. "And the reason I'm not going to be marrying Craig is because I'm going to be marrying you."

"Right."

Melanie's smile vanished. "Wrong," she said hoarsely.

She turned to face the dashboard, her stomach tightening to the point of pain. She suppressed a groan.

"Oh, no, Mel, I'm right as rain." He reached over to take her hand and ran a callused thumb over her sensitive palm. "You see, I have every intention of becoming your husband tomorrow."

Husband. Marc.

She tugged her hand away. "Please…don't touch me."

He laughed, the robust sound making her stare at him as if he had gone insane. "No, that may be what you've been saying to Craig the last three months. Me? Admit it, Mel." He moved his hand to her leg and brushed it up the inside of her thigh. "Me, you can't get enough of."

Incredibly, she felt like opening herself to his touch.

Panic swelled sure and strong in her chest, chasing the air from her lungs. His repeating the words didn't make her understand his announcement any better. Marriage to Marc would be— A peculiar melting sensation flowed throughout her body. Marriage to Marc would be wonderfully exciting, unpredictable, impossible.

The emotional roller coaster she'd been on for the past two days provided all the proof she needed that marriage to Marc would be a disaster. He was by turns irresistibly handsome, foolishly inexplicable and ultimately irresponsible.

"Where are we going?" she whispered.

That made him move his hand away. "Someplace safe."

She tightly closed her eyes. "We're not going back to that, are we, Marc? We agreed we were partners in this." She forced herself to stop worrying her hands in her lap. She'd tried to get the ring off at the hotel, but it wouldn't budge past her first knuckle. Her fingers must have swollen more than she realized. "That means sharing information. That means I get just as much say in where we go as you do. Someplace safe just…well, it doesn't cut it right now."

"It's going to have to cut it because that's all I'm giving you."

She fervently battled hysteria. "We're partners—"

"That was before I found out you're carrying my child."

She stared at him, puzzled. "Your child?" she whispered. "A little over an hour ago, you didn't even know I was pregnant."

He gazed at her from under his eyebrows. "Okay, *our* child."

"Which brings us back to the partners thing."

He slowly shook his head again. "Oh, no, Mel. The way I see it, our roles now are completely bipolar. You—" he gently jabbed a finger against her collarbone "—are officially in charge of eating right, exercising, taking your vitamins and creating a healthy internal environment for our child."

Her anger flared. "Who in the hell died and named you ob-gyn?"

"The way I see it, your being pregnant gives me license to do a lot you might not be happy with, Mel." He grinned. "Anyway, those are your duties. Now my duties..." He flexed his hands against the steering wheel. "My most important duty is to maintain a healthy external environment. Namely, keeping you safe." He glanced at her. "Nine months of hard labor is the way things look right now."

"Five months," she corrected absently. "And I'm the one who's facing labor."

Marc wants to take care of me. She rubbed her forehead with a shaking hand. The thought was appealing in a sort of medieval sense. Me man, you woman. Wasn't that the way things used to be? And while women had come a long way, baby, they still had a long way to go. Sure, small concessions had been made. In wedding ceremonies, it was no longer, "I now pronounce you man and wife," and men were known to wash the occasional dish or two. She flicked a glance at Marc, admitting that he not only washed dishes, he could whip up a pretty good meal with the help of the microwave, frozen vegetables and a broiler.

She squeezed her eyes shut. What was she doing? While her view of the future had been knocked askew, it was dangerous to make room for Marc in it. She felt as if she was wandering through a dangerous daydream where being handcuffed—literally and otherwise—to Marc didn't seem like such a bad proposition.

She shifted on the seat as they put the D.C. suburbs behind them.

"We can't even agree on anything, Marc. What makes you think we could make a family work?"

His expression never faltered. "We'll make it work."

Then it occurred to her that Marc wasn't doing all this because he loved her. He was doing it because it was the right thing to do. Marrying her was a duty. A job. And one he thought he was up for.

Her heart expanded painfully.

No, for the good of her baby, she couldn't marry either Craig or Marc.

While Marc's heart might be in the right place, the signal got scrambled somewhere between his chest and his head.

I'M GOING TO BE a father. Marc waited for panic, for anger, to set in, but all he felt was this strange kind of weightlessness. *I'm going to be a father.*

He glanced over to Mel, twisting that rock around her finger. He wanted to tell her to take it off, wished he could replace it with the one in his pocket. But now didn't seem like the right time.

Okay, he admitted he hadn't been overly enthusiastic when they'd initially discussed how they felt about children a year or so ago. He grimaced. Who was he kidding? He'd adamantly said he wouldn't even consider having kids. And he hadn't.

Boy, in light of the day's events, did that seem a lifetime ago.

His reasons had been solid enough. Raised in a family of four other males, with a male who barely got passing grades as a father and was far in the hole when it came to mothering, he wasn't the only one of the McCoy bunch to decide children weren't in the cards. His decision had come as a result of a long, middle-of-the-night conversation with Connor after his youngest brother, David, had run away. It had taken them some eight hours to find him.

Marc acknowledged that it hadn't been David's running away that had upset him so much. It had been where the four-year-old had run to.

His brothers and father had been about to report his disappearance to the local authorities when they got a call from their closest neighbor, three miles up the road. They would have called sooner, they said, but they hadn't known David's real name because he was calling himself Grover, after his favorite *Sesame Street* character, and said he didn't have a home.

Pops had driven Connor and him over to pick David up. Only when they tried to pry him away from the family, who were having dinner, their little brother had kicked and screamed, insisting that this was his home. No one could blame him. The neat little family, complete with mother and father and other children, would be anyone's ideal.

The entire humbling experience had made Marc realize he'd had a heart. More importantly, he'd learned that same heart could be broken.

"Mel, what I said…you know, before you told me you were pregnant…"

She looked at him in that way that made him squirm. It was worse than facing a crowd of protesters while guarding the president.

"Well, you have to know I had no idea.…"

"I was pregnant?"

He nodded. "Right."

"No problem."

He glanced toward her, but she had turned to stare through the window.

He tried again. "I know I once said I never wanted to have children."

He watched as her chin quivered slightly.

"Well, I don't feel that way anymore."

She made a sniffing sound, then finally looked at him. "And how exactly *do* you feel, Marc?"

It wasn't the first time she'd asked the question. He

couldn't count the times he'd been caught on the wrong side of what he called her "put your feelings into words" game. Still, he knew he had to try or risk a whole lot more than a whack in the arm.

"Happy?" he said cautiously.

Her short burst of laughter dismayed him.

"What?" he asked, frowning.

She appeared as caught off guard as he did, and she quickly looked away. "The way you said 'happy' in the form of a question." She cleared her throat. "So, are you happy or not?"

He hesitated. Not because he didn't know how he felt. He was afraid of falling into a carefully laid trap. "Yes. Yes, I am."

She didn't answer, and he couldn't see enough of her face to see her response.

He grew tense. "You always told me I was never any good at putting my feelings into words, Mel," he said gruffly. "But I want to try to explain this one to you, if you'll hear me out."

She nodded, but still didn't look at him.

He trained his gaze on the road disappearing under the wheels of the Jeep. "Two days ago I didn't think there was a chance in hell of ever seeing you again." It had been a difficult realization. But with Mel's wedding date fast approaching, and without a clue how to get to her, he'd given up hope of repairing things between them.

"Then Hooker escaped," she said.

He nodded, then said, "No, no. I mean, yes, of course he escaped, but that's not what I'm working at."

He finally earned her attention. He didn't know if that was good or bad. What he did know was that he was quickly running out of road, and if there was anything to be said, he better say it now, because he might not get a chance later.

Spit it out, McCoy.

"I don't know what I'm trying to say," he grumbled,

ticked off at himself. "But I do know that when you told me you were pregnant...well, I know you and—that a year ago when we talked about having kids...well, I thought I didn't want any."

He chanced a glance in her direction.

Get to the point already, man, you're losing her.

He clenched the steering wheel tightly. "And when I found out you were marrying somebody else...it shocked me, you know?" He bit back a curse. "My gut reaction was that something had to be going on, but I had no idea it was..."

She turned to the window.

"No, don't turn away," he said urgently, touching her arm. He couldn't define why, but it was important he say this to her, important she understand.

He withdrew his hand and exhaled loudly. "What I'm trying to say to you, Mel, is that when you told me you were having my...our baby, I knew it meant you weren't only going to be a part of my life...." He swallowed. "But that you were going to stay that way for a long time to come." He released the wheel and turned his hands palms up. "And I...I was happier than I've been in a long, long time." He rubbed the back of his neck so hard his skin hurt. "Maybe ever."

The silence in the Jeep was deafening. Marc kept his gaze fixed on the road, afraid he'd screwed up again.

But when seconds dragged into minutes without a reaction, he gave in and finally looked at her.

And found her crying. "Aw, hell, Mel, don't go turning on the waterworks again."

She made a sniffling sound that made him groan. "That's the sweetest thing you've ever said to me."

Despite the stiff way he sat, a funny feeling exploded in his chest. An odd mixture of pride and hope. "Yeah, well," he murmured, wondering if his face was red. "I wouldn't recommend looking for me to do it again. That was hard enough for me to say and I...I don't know if I can do it again."

MELANIE REACHED OUT and took his hand, ignoring his prickly posture as she cupped his palm against her cheek. For a long, glorious moment, she reveled in the rough feel of his skin against her. Tears plopped over his fingers, but she didn't really care.

He grew more tense, and she smiled, aware of how much the admission had cost him. He was right. She had constantly accused him of keeping his thoughts and feelings from her. But if this was any example of what lay dormant inside him, then she hadn't given him nearly enough credit.

"Come on," he said, opening the glove compartment. "Somebody will think I hit you or something." He handed her a tissue.

She wiped her cheeks and blew her nose, laughing at his horrified expression.

"Hell, Mel, if you don't stop, I'm never going to say stuff like that again."

She whacked him on the arm as a fresh bout of tears sprang to her eyes. "Must be the hormones," she said, wondering at her extreme emotional reaction to his gruff confession.

The Jeep fishtailed as Marc screeched to a stop on the two-lane road, earning him a honk from the truck behind them. "Good Lord. Do you have to be sick?"

Melanie glanced through the back window. "What are you doing? You could have gotten us killed."

The truck pulled around them, honking once more as it passed.

"So you're okay, then?"

Melanie laughed. She was more than okay—she was euphoric, delirious, thrilled. Despite the knowledge that his confession wouldn't, couldn't lead them anywhere.

"I'm fine, Marc. Not every pregnant woman gets sick, you know."

His grimace was endearing. "No, I didn't know." He rubbed the back of his neck. Something she noticed he was doing often lately. "Why do I have the feeling there's a whole lot about this I'm not going to know?"

Melanie hid her smile and glanced through the window as he got under way, going noticeably slower. She appreciated the deep green of the tobacco fields, the patches of wild rhododendrons, the utter stillness of the land around them. Then it dawned on her where he must be taking her.

Sure enough, ten minutes later she spotted a buckshot-peppered sign announcing they were entering Manchester, Population 1,999. She craned her neck at a small diner, then stared at a bar and gawked at a cute general store with the requisite old man sitting on a rocking chair whittling.

Melanie's heart dipped into her stomach. He was taking her home.

ALONG WITH the initial jolt of excitement Marc had felt at the news of his impending fatherhood, fear twisted in his gut. What did he know about being a father? He'd never been around kids. Well, aside from his brothers.

Boy, am I ever going to catch hell for this one, he thought, envisioning those same four brothers.

Marc slowed to the speed limit, spotting Sheriff Percy Mathison sitting in his usual place on the outskirts of town waiting for speeders. He waved, and Percy waved back tersely, apparently upset he wasn't able to get another hefty contribution to the Manchester County coffers.

It was late afternoon, and everyone was either home or on their way. The general store had its share of customers, as did the diner, but it was the absence of Connor's car at the bar that made Marc wince. That meant Connor was either working late or he was already home. He sincerely hoped it was the former, because he really didn't need another run-in with his older brother right now.

"This is…nice," Mel said quietly.

Nice. Now there was a word. But it certainly couldn't be used to describe Manchester. Small, maybe. Perhaps even okay. But definitely not nice. He grew more uncomfortable the closer he got to the family house. He grimaced. Mel would take back her words the minute she got a gander at the McCoy place.

Set back from the road, the old, sprawling farmhouse looked ready for the wrecking ball. Then there was the barn. The instant he thought about it, it came hulking into view, little more than a haunted, weatherworn, gargantuan structure whose slats had shifted long ago. It was no safer to enter than it looked. Not that it mattered. They hadn't had any animals in a long, long time. Unless you counted Mitch's dog Goliath. Even when his quarry darted inside, Goliath stood outside and barked up a storm. The old slobber puss never went in.

Marc shifted, nearly knocking his knee against the dash. He wasn't sure why he'd never brought Mel here, but as they approached, a prickly knot pulled tight in his stomach. He glanced over to find her attention glued to the scenery. No matter how she might react to the McCoy place, it was too late to turn back. Besides, it was the safest place for Mel and the…baby. No one would dare mess with the McCoys. No one.

He groaned when he spotted the cars parked in the rutted drive. It figured—every single McCoy male was home. While it meant more protection for Mel, it also meant a hell of a lot more trouble for him.

In all the years he'd lived here, not one of his brothers—or his father, for that matter—had ever brought a woman to visit. The youngest, David, had posted a sign on the front porch when he was six and had been burned by his first-grade girlfriend. It had said, No Girlz Allowed. Marc cringed when he saw the unvarnished piece of wood still hanging there, creaking ominously in the spring breeze.

Wait! Marc's black mood lightened as he brought the Jeep to a stop, blocking in everyone else. Mitch had brought a woman home once. Liz something or other. His hope deflated when he remembered that on the day of their wedding, Liz had run off, leaving Mitch standing high and dry at the altar.

"This is home?" Mel asked quietly, her eyes huge as she took in the overgrown grass, the drooping fence, the demolished front steps.

"Yep. This is it."

He climbed from the Jeep, sensing rather than seeing Mel step to his side. He cleared his throat. "The place isn't usually this…" He coughed, catching the lie before he finished it. Of course the place was usually this bad.

Marc spotted Connor looking out the side door. He was filled with a sudden urge to hustle Mel into the Jeep but managed to hold his ground.

He exhaled. "Guess we'd better get this over with. Come on."

He wasn't sure what Mel had expected, but when he realized she wasn't next to him, he looked to find her frowning at his back before reluctantly following.

"Aw, hell." He backtracked and held his arm for her to take.

She kept her hands stoically at her sides. "I'm okay."

"Take my arm, Mel."

Her eyes flashed. "I said I'm okay. Pregnant women can walk on their own."

He bit back a curse and grabbed her stiff, cold hand. "Why does everything have to be a fight with you?" He noticed he'd quickened his step and purposely slowed it. "Oh, and about the, um…"

"Baby?"

"Yeah, the pregnancy thing. Let's say we keep that information to ourselves for a while, okay?" He didn't want to send his father into cardiac arrest. "Anyway, I think it's a good idea if we tell them we're getting married first."

She tried to pull her hand away. He held fast.

"Marc McCoy, I'm not going to marry you."

"Sure, Mel, sure," he said, decidedly distracted.

JUST WHEN SHE THOUGHT Marc had passed some major milestone, he'd say or do something that completely destroyed it. Now was no exception.

"Marc, I—"

He grimaced at her. "We'll talk about this later, okay?"

"Okay."

"Good."

She looked at him long and hard. Was it her, or was Marc McCoy anxious? She noted the way his mouth was pulled into a nervous line, no trace of the happiness he'd proclaimed a short time ago. She followed his gaze. Someone stood at the side door. They were similar in size and hair coloring, but that's where the similarities ended. One of Marc's brothers? It seemed the obvious guess. As they drew closer, she saw the glum expression on the other man's face, and knew for sure that it had to be true. Only a blood relative of Marc could pull off that don't-screw-with-me look.

"Marc," he said.

"Connor."

Melanie waited for an introduction, but not for long. Marc pulled her inside the house with barely enough time for her to make eye contact with Connor.

For a ridiculous moment, she was afraid he intended to take her inside and stuff her in a closet away from his family, away from where she might get him or herself into any trouble. He pulled her into the kitchen. She stopped cold, her breath freezing somewhere en route between her lungs and her nose.

Oh, God.

Marc finally released her hand, leaving her standing in

the doorway, barely aware when Connor gently budged her out of the way so he could pass and join the room full of other McCoy males.

The house had appeared enormous from the outside. But looking at it now, filled to the brim with prime male flesh, she didn't think there was a house large enough to hold the amount of testosterone in the room.

"Hi," she said hoarsely.

10

MELANIE WAS AFRAID she had spoken a foreign language. No one responded to her choked greeting. Her gaze slowly drifted over five devastatingly handsome faces. They stared back. Despite the size of the table, which could easily fit a family of ten, it looked puny with these guys sitting at it.

Suddenly, everyone spoke at once. But it was the oldest, maybe Marc's father, who rose.

Melanie blinked slowly. It couldn't be. It wasn't possible. "Sean?"

His grizzly warm grin told her it could be and was. Then it dawned on her. Sean hadn't been at the hospital to visit anyone else, as she had assumed. He had never corrected her. Sean was Marc's father.

A missing puzzle piece shifted into place, completing a picture she hadn't known was there. All at once, she recalled how he had defended Marc's actions, offered practical reasons Marc hadn't come to visit her. At the time, she hadn't thought it odd that he should try to defend someone he didn't know. She thought it was a man thing.

"Maybe he can't get away from work," Sean had suggested.

When that one hadn't worked during their third visit— when he'd smuggled in eggs, bacon and hash browns from a nearby family restaurant because she wasn't eating the hospital fare—he'd said quietly, "Maybe there's something about hospitals that bothers him."

When she had quietly disagreed, he had gone on.

"I don't think it's so far-fetched. This is the first time

I've...well, that I've spent so much time in a hospital in a long, long time. You see, my wife died...."

Melanie's mind reeled with the images and words, her thoughts a jumble as she realized how much she knew about the family before her, though not through normal channels. During her long conversations with Sean while her mother had been busy ordering the hospital personnel around, while Craig had been working and Joanie had been snowed under at her shop, she and Marc's father had spent hours talking, seemingly about nothing. She had thought he was humoring her by telling her about himself. And even then she had wondered if what he was sharing was true, or was just a way to get her mind off her own problems.

She now knew every one of his stories had been true.

Her gaze drifted over the four other men in the room. She realized she could pick them out based on what Sean had told her.

The tall one who had been at the door had dark eyes that looked as though they had seen more than any one man should. He offered her a chair. She would have known without Marc's calling him by name that he was Connor. Sean had said Connor had been more of a father to the others than he had ever been. It appeared he was still playing the role. She sat down and murmured a thank-you.

Then it occurred to her that Sean knew an awful lot about her. She felt her cheeks go hot, remembering all she'd shared with him, thinking him a stranger she could confide in with no risk of her troubles becoming known to anybody else.

"Evening, Mellie. You'll have to excuse us," Sean said with a grin Melanie realized was reminiscent of Marc's. "We're not used to having women around here."

Shocker, Melanie thought, and returned his smile.

"Can I talk to you in the other room for a minute?" Connor said to Marc.

Panic swelled in Melanie's throat. *No.* Marc couldn't leave her here with…with *them.* She could barely manage him—if that's what you could call what she did with him—much less four other brothers exactly like him. Well, not exactly like him. One of the brothers had sandy blond hair. One of them looked as though he had missed his last two appointments at the barbershop. But given their gift for gab so far—

Sean put a hand on her shoulder, seeming to sense her uneasiness. She instantly relaxed. "Are you hungry? Here, why don't I fix you a plate."

She slowly shook her head, feeling a little better. "No, really, I'm not—"

"I already fixed her one, Pops." Marc plopped a plate full of meat loaf, mashed potatoes and corn in front of her. Her stomach growled. A quiet laugh next to her said she wasn't the only one who heard it. She looked to find the blond brother—a dead ringer for Brad Pitt—watching her. He would be David, she realized.

"Excuse us for a minute, will you?" Connor said, aiming a grin at her. He slapped a hand against Marc's back and moved it toward his neck. The way Marc bent slightly told Melanie he didn't have much choice in the matter.

She hid her smile and watched the one with long dark hair—he would be Mitch, ex-FBI, now PI—as he put a glass of milk in front of her.

"You must be Melanie," he said, sitting down.

She nodded and filled her fork with potatoes.

"Nice to meet you. I'm Mitch."

A chair screeched as the blond one scooted closer. "I'm David. And the quiet one over there is Jake. Don't let him scare you. He's probably wondering if you have your green card."

That's right. Marc had told her once that all his brothers were in law enforcement. The information combined with what Sean had shared gave her a jumping off point. "That must make him the one with Immigration and Naturalization Services."

"And do you?" Jake asked.

She choked. "Excuse me?"

"Have your green card."

She laughed. "Better. I have a copy of my birth certificate."

He didn't respond.

"Showing I was born here."

David chuckled. "Don't pay him any mind. He's just yanking your chain."

Popping a bite of meat loaf into her mouth, she considered him. "Let's see, you're David, so that must make you with the police department."

"Right."

She gestured toward the table. "Please, eat."

"She's right," Sean said, and sat down. "We're making her uncomfortable."

"No, really, you're not," she lied. "Food just tastes better with company."

She saw Mitch topping up her glass with more milk and Sean putting more meat loaf on her plate. Then it hit her. The reason everyone had responded so unusually to her when she came in. Why Connor had quickly offered a chair, why Mitch had poured her milk instead of soda or beer, why Sean, David and Mitch were hovering over her like a trio of mother hens. Devastatingly handsome, testosterone-laden mother hens.

She fearfully sought out Sean.

His shy grin told her he knew exactly what she had just realized. "Sorry, Mellie. But I couldn't keep, well, you know, the secret once we got word Marc had made off with you."

The mashed potatoes stuck to the roof of her mouth. Marc didn't have to worry about telling his family anything about the baby. They already knew.

"You don't look pregnant," David said next to her.

Mitch swatted him on the arm. "Are there any vitamins or anything you should be taking? Would you like some water to wash them down with?"

"I'm fine—"

"You look tired," Jake said in the same accusatory tone he'd used when inquiring about her green card. "Maybe you should lie down after you eat."

"I'm fine, really, I am." Melanie was unsure how to react to the onslaught of male attention.

David pushed her plate closer to her. "Eat before it gets cold."

Melanie managed another forkful. "Um, Sean, I don't remember you telling me exactly what you do for a living."

Connor came into the room and patted his father's arm. "Pops here is still walking the beat for the D.C. Police Department." He reached across the table. Melanie quickly wiped her hand on her napkin and shook his hand. Was it her imagination, or had he cringed at the pressure of her shake? "Sorry I was rude. I'm Connor. That house Marc holed you up in last night is the property of the U.S. Marshal's office."

She nearly choked. David handed her the glass of milk. Jake moved his chair a little farther away. "You mean it was a government safe house?"

"Uh-huh."

Speaking of Marc, where was he? Melanie glanced nervously toward the door.

"He'll be back in a minute," Connor said. "He wanted to…clean up a bit."

Clean up? She wasn't aware he'd been dirty. Her mind provided a vivid image of their shower together mere hours ago.

She had finished half the plate of food when Marc finally reappeared. He looked none too happy. And the red smudge under his right cheekbone told her why.

"Oh, God!" She jumped to her feet and hurried to him, ignoring his protests.

"He's got and given lots worse than that, Mel," Jake said.

She was growing angrier by the second. She swiveled toward the table full of men, including Marc in her disbelieving sights. "Is that the reason you two left the room? To get into a fistfight?"

Marc tugged on her shirtsleeve. "Uh, Mel—"

She shrugged him off and looked at Connor.

"Just a bit of payback for the shove I took this morning," he said.

"This morning? You mean you came to the safe house?"

He nodded and rubbed his knuckles. His wince made her cringe.

Marc cleared his throat. "Mel, I think we'd better—"

She ignored him and visually swept the rest of the table. "And all of you knew what was going on when they left the room?"

"Mel—"

She shushed him.

The way the McCoy males instantly avoided her gaze told her they'd known and hadn't done a thing to stop it from happening. She supposed she should be glad they spared her from seeing the exchange.

"I can't believe this. Is this the way you settle problems between each other? A shove here, a punch there?" She shook her head. "Haven't any of you heard of verbal communication?"

Jake caught her attention as he scratched his chin. "What better way to let each other know you're royally pissed then a punch in the jaw?"

She planted her hands on her hips and stared at each of them in turn. "I sincerely hope none of you act this way on the job."

They all denied that at once. Melanie wanted to put her

hands to her ears as she turned toward Marc. "Did you really hit Connor this morning?"

"I didn't hit him, I...well, I kind of pushed him and he, um, he fell down the stairs. Can we go in the other room now, please?"

"Apologize."

Marc blinked at her. "What?"

A quiet chuckle came from the table. Melanie turned toward the culprit. David looked away.

"I said apologize to Connor. Now."

"Hell, Mel, he already got in his lick—"

She grabbed his hand and tugged him across the room toward his older brother. "Shake."

Connor looked at Marc's hand, his arms crossed stoically. Melanie raised an eyebrow. He cleared his throat and reluctantly took his brother's hand.

Marc remained silent. Melanie elbowed him in the ribs. He mumbled contritely. "Sorry, Connor."

"For what?" she prompted.

"Aw, come on, Mel—" He sighed. "I'm sorry for shoving you and taking your gun when you came by this morning. It's just—"

Melanie slapped her hand over the mouth she had thoroughly kissed a short time ago, feeling the heat of his flesh against her palm. "There's no justifying when you apologize."

The two men dropped hands, both looking enormously uncomfortable.

"Now we can leave the room," she said.

Marc stared at her. "What about Connor? Doesn't he owe me an apology?"

Melanie nearly laughed at his boyishly offended expression. "I don't have any control over what Connor does or doesn't do, Marc."

She caught a glimpse of Sean, who sat on two chair legs, grinning. He winked at her, and she felt herself blush from head to foot.

Who'd have thought she had *that* in her? Certainly not her. More of her mother must have rubbed off on her than she realized. Or maybe her impending motherhood had set off some sort of gene she hadn't been aware she had. Either way, she felt oddly at peace with herself…and at ease.

I KNEW there was a reason I never brought her here, Marc thought. It had been more than the fear of what she'd think of the place. More than being afraid she'd take the move the wrong way. He'd somehow known she wouldn't understand him and his brothers.

He followed Mel as she led the way into the living room. His gaze was glued to her nicely rounded backside. It had been a long time since he'd seen her in a pair of jeans. And these ones did her bottom proud.

He turned on a light as she turned toward him, no doubt to give him what for. But while he still wasn't entirely clear on what had happened in there, he hadn't yet lost the ability to knock her off track.

"Now, before you go getting your panties in a twist, you should know Connor and I did more than go at each other in here." He held her gaze. "I had Connor scour the beach for one of the bullets this morning."

He watched the wind slowly disappear from her sails as she blinked.

"He handed it over to David, who had D.C. ballistics compare it with the one you, um, took three months ago." He cleared his throat. "Perfect match."

She stood still for a long moment, then sat on the edge of the sofa. "So trading shoves and punches isn't the only thing you and your brothers are capable of."

He grinned. "Honestly, that doesn't happen often." He ran his fingers through his hair. "I think the last time Connor and I came to blows was over a decade ago."

"Over what?"

He shrugged, then turned and sat in his father's recliner. "I wrapped his Goat around a tree that used to be in the front yard."

"You hurt an animal?"

"No, no. The Goat is a car. A GTO."

Her answering smile warmed him all over. "Yes, I'd say that would deserve a punch or two."

He crossed his arms, affecting nonchalance, when inside his every muscle tensed. "He broke my jaw in two places."

He watched her horrified expression. Her gaze dropped to his jawline. He figured sharing that was enough. She didn't have to know the rest. How his father and Connor had dragged him into the emergency room. How he'd fought the intern and ended up strapped to a gurney. His throat tightened unbearably. How a school bus had been involved in an accident at the same time and in all the excitement, he'd been forgotten, left by himself for four and half hours, untreated, next to a young boy they hadn't been able to revive.

Her soulful eyes lifted to his. "You sent Sean to the hospital, didn't you?"

He hadn't expected the question and didn't quite know how to respond. "Yes," he said quietly.

"Why didn't you come yourself?"

He hated the lump in his throat. "I...I couldn't, Mel. I just couldn't."

His gut twisted into knots. He hated his weakness when it came to hospitals. But this late in the game, he supposed there wasn't much either he or anybody else could do about it. If he couldn't bring himself to go in when Mel was shot...

"Does it have anything to do with your mother?"

He coughed. "Pops told you about that, huh?"

She nodded slowly, not helping him. He figured he deserved it. She was completely right in her argument that he didn't share enough of himself, his past, his thoughts, with her. It wasn't because he didn't want her to know. It was just that he didn't think the words worth saying. Who cared if he nearly hyperventilated—him, two hundred pounds of prime secret service agent—every time he spotted a hospital? What did it matter that his mother had died when he was young? Lots of children lost one or sometimes both of their parents and still managed okay. Mel had grown up without a father.

He realized she was still waiting for an answer. He gave her the only one he had. "I associate hospitals with death, Mel." His thick swallow sounded loud in the room. "I couldn't have stood it if I lost you in one, too."

He looked away, hating that his eyes burned, hating that she looked at him in that pitying way. "Sorry, that came out a little rougher than I meant it to. I'm not used to talking about, well, you know, feelings." He clamped his hands together. "I guess being raised in an all-female household has its advantages," he said carefully.

Mel's gaze was soft. "Trust me, Joanie and I had our fights, but they usually involved destruction of clothing."

He welcomed his unexpected laugh, but the smile had vanished from her face. Before he knew it, she had crossed to him, threading her fingers through his hair and forcing him to look up. Giving in to the need to feel her, he laid his head against her belly, finding it amazing that in there somewhere beat the heart of their child. A child they had created together.

Mel would make a wonderful mother, he realized. She would be strong and witty as well as loving and nurturing. He could already see her singing the baby to sleep in the middle of the night. Imagine her coaxing the toddler to eat food he disliked. Hugging the child when he came home after having been teased at school. He saw all of this.

And he wanted to be a part of it so bad it hurt.

She slowly drew away. "So," she said quietly. "Now that we know Hooker is the one who shot at me this morning, where do we go from here?"

He cleared his throat. "We don't go anywhere, Mel."

She looked at him for a long time. "Don't you even—"

He held up his hand to stop her. "David's already passed on the information to those who need to know it."

She stood a little straighter. Marc's gaze was drawn to her stomach. He didn't know if it was fact or if he was imagining it because he knew she was pregnant, but he swore he could make out the new fullness of her belly.

"Was he able to get any other information on Hooker?" she asked. "Have the authorities checked out his house? His sister's place? Staked out all his usual hangouts in case he surfaces?"

He nodded. "They've done and are doing all that, Mel."

She turned and started pacing. He grimaced. The whole point of bringing her here was to make her feel safe. It wasn't going to help if she insisted on being a part of things.

She abruptly faced him. "You already have a plan, don't you?"

He didn't respond.

"And you're not going to let me in on it, are you?"

He wasn't sure if he liked where this was heading.

"God, this really stinks, you know, McCoy?"

He grinned. "Better watch out. You're in a house with six McCoys now."

She looked toward the kitchen, her palm going to her forehead as she considered what he said. When she looked at him, he could see she was still angry, but she was also undeniably concerned. "I'm putting my life…the life of our baby in your hands, Marc. Please take care of us."

For the first time in his life Marc knew what absolute fear felt like. "I will."

MELANIE LEANED against the kitchen counter, trying to sort out the details of her life. Despite the newfound closeness between her and Marc, she couldn't envision a future for them together. The whole marriage thing... She swallowed hard. Well, she would just have to straighten that out once the threat that loomed over her head was gone.

An odd warmth spread through her chest. She had to give the guy credit, though. Marc McCoy was a boyish adventurer ninety-nine percent of the time, but when it came down to the important things, he did the right thing. Both by her and the baby.

If only he could give her what she yearned for most—his love.

She idly watched as David rinsed then loaded plates in what had to be the biggest dishwasher they made. She glanced around the room. In fact, it was probably the only appliance that had been bought within the past ten years. An old commercial-size refrigerator hummed in the corner, and she was afraid that if she looked more closely at the six-burner stove, she'd find it had a compartment for wood.

She reached for a towel and absently folded it, hating that she didn't know what was going on in the other room, where the remainder of the McCoy males were discussing her future. But she knew giving in to Marc was a wise choice. For three months she'd based her decisions on what was best for her baby. Now that her existence was threatened, this was probably the most important thing she could ever do for her child. Especially since she couldn't marry his father.

At least she'd been given phone privileges. Marc had loomed over her, but he hadn't interfered while she let her family know she was all right.

Her gaze wandered to the door.

"Do they do this often?" she asked David.

"What? Call family meetings?" He gave her a half grin, reminding her again of how very much he looked like Brad Pitt. "No."

Melanie looked at him closely. He couldn't be more

than a shade over thirty—her age—if that, but his blue eyes reflected the wisdom of a sixty-year-old. *Good, a McCoy who doesn't feel he has to wisecrack his way through everything.*

She turned to the counter and folded her hands on top of it, pretending an interest in the sunset she could see through the window overlooking the back yard. *Back yard?* It seemed as if half of Virginia stretched behind the McCoy house, crisscrossed with sagging fences.

"Do you mind if I ask you a question?" David said.

She glanced at him. "Shoot." She grimaced, thinking she'd seen enough shooting to last her a lifetime, thank you very much.

"I...I'm having a few women problems."

Women problems? Melanie battled against a smile and lost. "Sorry." She motioned with her hands and returned her attention to the sunset. Only *she* would find herself on the brink of a conversation regarding someone else's love life. "I don't think I'm exactly an expert on male-female relationships." *That was an understatement.* "But I'll do the best I can."

He didn't say anything, and she turned to him. He was scratching at something on the edge of a plate. His hands were long and lean, and he looked so deep in thought, Melanie felt the inexplicable urge to know what was on his mind.

She quietly cleared her throat. "This woman. Have you known her long?"

"Only a few weeks." He put the plate in the dishwasher and closed it. "She's my partner. That's why I thought talking to you about my predicament might help."

Melanie worried her bottom lip, wondering exactly how much he knew about her and Marc.

David piled the pans in the sink.

"Here," she said, pushing away from the counter. "Let me get those."

He grinned. "I could hold my ground with the dishes,

but you could get yourself in trouble offering to do these." He glanced toward the door. "Only don't tell anyone I let you do anything more than sit at the table. They'd have my hide."

She laughed and pushed him gently out of the way. It might help if she had something to do while she waited for Marc. She didn't mind helping David with his problem. If he ever got around to sharing it.

Then it occurred to her that she had some bargaining power. David wanted advice on his love life. She wanted, needed to know more about Marc.

David reached into a cupboard, took out a mug, then poured a cup of coffee.

"Before you go on," she said, filling a couple of the messier pans with hot water and soap and putting them aside, "I'd like to make a deal with you."

"Deal?" He pushed a lock of golden hair from his forehead.

"Yeah. I answer your questions, then you can answer some of mine."

He eyed her over the rim of his cup. "Ah, Marc's a bit of a mystery man."

She smiled. "A bit."

"I don't know if I can help because we haven't been able to figure him out yet either, but..." He gave her a crooked grin. "It's a deal."

"Good." She rinsed a pan and put it in the drainer. "You first."

He pondered for a minute while she poured half a can of cleanser into a stainless steel skillet.

"Tell me, Mel, what is it that women really want?"

Melanie dropped the cleanser in the sink, then scrambled to pick it up. Why did she have the feeling answering David's question wasn't going to be as easy as she thought?

11

MARC TURNED OVER yet again, tempted to punch the floor to make it softer. If only it had a chance in hell of working, he would have. He threw his head against the pillow and winced, knowing being away from Melanie was as much to blame for his agitated state as his sleeping arrangements on the floor of Mitch's bedroom.

"Can I ask you a question, Mitch?"

The bedsprings squeaked. Marc looked at his brother, as comfortable as you please in the double bed. "Hmm?"

"Why are you such an awful host?"

Mitch's chuckle grated on his nerves. "You were the one who went and made an ass of yourself by tossing and turning and got kicked out of the bed, not me."

Marc sighed and draped his arm across his head. "Good thing that's not my question, then, isn't it?"

The springs squeaked again, and Mitch squinted at him through the darkness. "Will you just ask your question already so I can get some sleep?"

Marc grimaced. "Yeah, life must be pretty tough as a clientless PI."

"I have clients. I'm just taking a bit of a leave, that's all," Mitch corrected. "Anyway, I meant we both need our sleep if we're to keep up with this rigid schedule we came up with to keep a constant watch on the house."

"Yeah, you're right." Marc lay back, reviewing what he, his father and brothers had worked out earlier in the evening.

First had come the objectives. Keeping Mel safe was definitely at the top of the list. He really didn't want to think about how they knew she was pregnant, but they all did. The best he could figure, Mel must have told his old man a lot more in that hospital than Pops had let on.

Second was to catch Hooker so he could never prove a threat to her again. In conjunction with the first objective, all five brothers had agreed to take two-hour watches until Hooker was caught, with Pops staying in the house as the final barrier between Hooker and Mel.

To see through the second objective, Marc had put the word out on his and Mel's whereabouts. If Hooker wanted her, Hooker would have to go through the McCoys to get her.

He frowned. His only concern now was his inability to get through to his partner, Roger Westfield. He wasn't on the schedule for post duty and he hadn't answered his phone, leaving Marc to believe he was out with one of his many dates.

The only obvious drawback to the plan was that it would soon eliminate the reason Mel was with him. As much as he'd like to believe in his ability to convince her to marry him, he knew it was far from a done deal. And if she went back to Bedford and started working at her new, cushy position, his job would be very tough, if not downright impossible.

Marc stretched his neck and swallowed hard. He'd never really talked about relationship stuff with any of his brothers. Well, not anything that went beyond comparing been-there, done-that lists, anyway. And just because he needed some information didn't necessarily mean he'd find anything out. Especially since given the subject of his question, Mitch was more liable to slug him than answer him.

He cleared his throat. "Mitch, do you remember, oh, I don't know." He hedged, thinking about chucking the whole question. "Seven years ago."

Mitch was unusually quiet. There was no squeak of the bedsprings, no noticeable sign of his breathing.

Marc pressed on. "What I want to know is, do you, you know, ever regret not going after her?"

When the silence dragged on, Marc lifted himself on one elbow, wondering if he should have said her name. He lay down. No. Out of all of them, Mitch had been the only one tempted to try the marriage route. He'd gotten as far as the altar before Liz Braden stood him up. There was no way a guy forgot something like that.

"Yes."

The word filled the room but sounded oddly far away. Marc rubbed the back of his neck, wondering where his brother was right now. Here? Or somewhere out there with Liz?

"No."

Marc frowned and sat up, staring over the side of the mattress at the empty bed. Where did he go? Then he realized Mitch must have climbed out the window and onto the roof over the front porch. He'd done it often when they were younger, earning him his share of ribbing for being what they all saw as a dreamer.

Marc sat on the bed and looked out the window. He wasn't about to go out there after him. He'd done it once as a teen and nearly got tossed over the side for his efforts. "That roof is going to collapse on you one of these days, you know."

Mitch stretched his jeans-clad legs in front of him, his back against the house. "Let it."

Marc grimaced and looked out at stars. There were so many of them. "So you didn't tell me which was your answer, yes or no."

Mitch crossed his arms over his bare chest. "Both, I guess." The night was dark, the only sound the crickets. "I would have liked an explanation why, I guess." His deep swallow was audible. "But at the same time, my damn pride wouldn't let me go after it, you know?"

"Yeah, I know."

"Anyway, that's muddy water under a bridge that

washed out a long time ago." Mitch shifted to look at him. "Why do you ask?"

Marc shrugged. "I don't know. Just curious, I guess."

"Curious, my ass. What's going on in that head of yours, Marc?"

Marc moved to his makeshift bed on the floor, pondering what Mitch had said and ignoring his question.

"You know," Mitch said, his voice muffled, "I'm surprised you haven't tried to sneak into the room down the hall yet."

Marc grew agitated and punched his pillow. "The old man hasn't started snoring yet."

Mitch's laugh threatened to wake the whole household. Marc picked up his pillow and tossed it out the window.

MELANIE HAD BEEN afraid they'd never leave her alone. Jake had brought her a thicker blanket—though the room was so hot she could barely stand the sheet. David had brought her a nubby blue terry robe. Mitch had asked if she wanted to talk about anything, to which she had smiled and said no. Sean had brought her some milk and cookies, then knocked on the door every five minutes until a half hour ago, asking her if she was okay.

Finally, blessedly alone, Melanie snuggled into the single bed and filled her nose with the smell of Marc all around her. Marc's bed. Marc's pillow. Marc's sports trophies reflecting the moonlight from a shelf on the wall. She smiled and rolled over, more content than she suspected was safe. But since no one was looking, there was no harm in indulging in the connection to the father of her child.

She'd enjoyed it when Sean had made it clear she and Marc were not to share a room. Marc had argued, but to no avail. Especially when his four brothers had joined in and agreed that there should be no sinful shenanigans under the McCoy roof. Even though her pregnancy was proof that they'd indulged in plenty outside the McCoy house.

Sinful shenanigans.

She gave a little shiver of anticipation, for the first time really seeing what life was going to be like with a baby in it.

She glanced at the clock, knowing there was no way Marc wasn't going to violate his father's dictate. In fact, she'd expected him to sneak into the room long before now. Where was he? She rolled over and sighed, wondering if maybe he'd fallen to sleep in Mitch's room.

The way she understood it, the only McCoys who still lived in the house were Sean and now Mitch. He'd moved back shortly before David had moved out. Marc, Connor, Jake and David all lived in D.C. or the suburbs, for convenience. But all of them called this old house home, and returned as often as they could, usually Wednesday nights and weekends, sharing meals, probably shooting the breeze and likely holding on to all that bonded them together.

Melanie sobered. Given what Marc had grudgingly shared with her while they were alone in the living room, what David had haltingly told her in the kitchen and what she had learned from Sean, she knew the glue that bonded them together was of the super adhesive type.

She didn't know all the details, but from what she understood, Marc's mother had died during childbirth some twenty-eight years earlier, when David was two. She worried her bottom lip, calculating that Marc would have been five. David said he couldn't remember anything about her but her scent. The rest of the brothers recalled bits and pieces, and Connor was good about sharing memories with them all since he was the oldest.

Connor had taken on the role of father when Sean had been helpless to stop himself from sinking into a depression so black he'd sometimes disappear for days, leaving the five young boys to fend for themselves.

She stilled her hand where it lay flat against her belly, swearing she felt movement just beneath the surface. Her doctor had told her she should start becoming aware of the baby's movements some time during her fourth month. After long, quiet moments with no further sensation, she thought she must have imagined it.

She shifted restlessly, hurting for Sean but most of all hurting for Marc because he remembered his mother and more than likely had memories of her being pregnant. In her mind's eye, she saw this precocious five-year-old touching his mother's belly, excited and challenged by the life growing inside her. A life extinguished along with his mother's.

Melanie swallowed tears, her hands touching her belly, remembering how protective Marc was of her. She guessed a lot of his behavior stemmed from his childlike pride and his admitted fear of never seeing her again. But she now understood a hefty measure came from losing not only his mother, but also his baby sister, when he was so young.

The floorboards outside her door squeaked. She sat instantly upright, her heart thundering in her chest as she reached for the revolver on the nightstand. Cocking it, she pointed it at the wooden barrier.

Slowly, the doorknob turned. She waited, holding her breath, her finger surprisingly calm where it rested against the trigger.

Marc.

Exhaling, she dropped the .22 to her lap and rolled her eyes heavenward. "You scared the daylights out of me," she said.

"Shh." Marc peered down the hall, then quietly closed the door. "I thought the old man would never go to sleep."

The fear that Hooker had somehow gained access to the house diminishing, Melanie put her gun, which Marc had given back to her, on the nightstand. She remembered

Sean's stern warning before they'd retired to their rooms—all except Jake, who'd stayed on in the kitchen—and fought a smile. She felt as if she was in high school and her boyfriend had just thrown a stone at the window. Only Marc probably would have broken the window, she thought, smiling.

"Move over," he said, lifting the sheet.

"I thought you'd never ask." Scooting over as far as she could on the single bed, Melanie sighed contentedly when he climbed in behind her, spooning her against his warm length. "Nice," she murmured.

How long had it been since Marc had held her? Just held her? Never, she realized. There was really never a time when they had snuggled for the pure pleasure of snuggling.

And you shouldn't get used to it now, either, a voice inside her warned.

Pushing aside all the questions that demanded answers she wasn't yet prepared to give, she reached behind her.

"Mm, even nicer."

Marc trapped her hand in his, his voice low. "Stop it, you tease."

She raised her eyebrows in the dark. "Stop it?" That's the second time Marc had put off her seduction attempts. She must be losing her touch.

She shifted, causing the bedsprings to squeak.

"Quiet, or you'll wake the ogre who lives down the hall."

She laughed. "I wouldn't call him an ogre."

She made out his grimace in the moonlight that drifted in from the window above the headboard.

"You didn't have to grow up with him."

She ran her fingers along his smooth jaw, remembering it had once been broken. "I'd trade you my mother for your father any day."

His chuckle shook the mattress. "No, thanks."

She listlessly moved her hand to his chest. She was

used to him wearing nothing to bed, but out of consideration for their surroundings, he wore a pair of boxer shorts. She let her fingers dip lower across the velvety skin of his stomach, reveling in his low hiss.

He caught her hand in his again. "I said stop it, Mel."

She leaned over and kissed him, slowly, thoroughly, loving the taste of toothpaste on his tongue. She closed her eyes and pressed her nose against his. "Your reluctance wouldn't have anything to do with my…condition, would it?"

She felt rather than saw his grin. "Condition?"

She took his hand. "Ever since finding out I'm pregnant, you've been treating me with kid gloves." She kissed him again, a moan building in her throat as he willingly let his fingers be led to her wetness. "There isn't any need to. I'm perfectly capable of having a normal sex life until I'm well into the third trimester."

This time he kissed her, and she could sense the urgency lurking behind a thin barrier of caution. "Are you sure?"

She nodded.

No longer in need of her talents as a guide, he flicked the tip of his finger over her pressure point, causing her to shudder in pleasure. She tightly grasped his biceps and laughed. "Hmm, I'd say you adjust quickly."

She moved to push him on the mattress and nearly succeeded in toppling him from the bed. She laughed, and he pressed a finger against her lips as he righted himself beneath her.

"Keep up the chatter, Mel, and you'll end up spending the rest of the night alone."

She tugged her T-shirt off and let it drop to the floor, pleased when he cupped her breasts. "Now that would be a real shame, wouldn't it?"

She arched into his touch, loving the feel of his palms against her breasts and the way he feathered his thumbs over her nipples, causing them to ache.

There was something decidedly sinful about making love to Marc in his family's house, with his brothers and father just down the hall. She cradled Marc's erection between her thighs, causing him to groan. She quickly covered his mouth with her hand. He nipped at her skin with his teeth, and she pulled back, laughing quietly.

She'd long accused Marc of being a breast man, and he obviously intended to prove her point now. She shivered, not about to stop the thorough attention, reveling in the texture of his tongue, the flick of his thumb, the squeeze of his fingers, knowing that the complete passion behind his actions was more responsible for the flames licking inside her than his touch.

His movements slowed, and he lay back. She could feel him watching her. When he spoke, his voice was quiet. "David told me that you and he had a long talk earlier."

Melanie stilled the rocking of her hips. She tried to make out his features and covered his hands where he was still touching her. "Yes. Yes, we did."

"He said you weren't going to marry me."

She touched his cheek, running her fingers along the fine line of his jaw.

There was so much Melanie wanted to explain to him, so much she wanted to say, but now wasn't the time. She couldn't help fearing that there wouldn't be a time, that the opportunity for them to discuss such intimate matters had already passed. And that scared her even more than the man hunting her.

"Let's not talk about that now, okay?"

Slowly, she bent toward him, pressing her mouth against his, communicating her feelings and urging him to share his. When he buried his fingers in her hair and languidly returned her kiss, she knew this time she wouldn't be denied.

MELANIE SLOWLY AWOKE to a cardinal calling outside the window. She stretched, aware of the thoroughly sated condition of her body. She reached out, only to realize she was the only one in the small bed.

Propping herself up, she pushed back one of the curtains to peer outside. The purple smears across the eastern sky told her it was very near dawn. Somewhere around five, Marc had left her, murmuring something about his turn at taking watch. She scanned the grounds but saw no sign of him.

She eased down on the bed, her contentment slowly seeping away no matter how hard she tried to hold on to it.

Over the past three days it had been all too easy to let her plans for the future fade to the background. When faced with the urgency of her present situation, it was no wonder. Out there somewhere, Hooker was waiting in the shadows.

But if everything Marc said was true, and if the trap he was setting for Hooker panned out, then the urgency would end and she would be smack-dab in the middle of the mess she'd made out of things.

She lay on her back, staring at the ceiling. Well, she hadn't exactly created a mess. Despite all that had happened, her blazing attraction for Marc and their very sinful shenanigans, not much had changed. She was still pregnant. And even though she knew she could never marry Craig, as far as everyone else was concerned, judging from her conversation with her mother the night before, she was still set to marry him in... She glanced at the clock. Six hours.

That sent her into a coughing fit.

Six hours?

She stared at the window. Marc had closed it—for safety reasons, he'd said. She knelt on the bed and pushed it open, needing some fresh air.

As she lay down, she mechanically counted off all the reasons she had once thought Craig would make a better husband and father than Marc. He was dependable. Stable. She knew him and he knew her better than anyone else. Outside work, they held much in common. He was thoughtful and loving and completely unselfish.

But all those were reasons he made a great friend.

His job doesn't require he put his life on the line.

She kicked off the covers. That point wasn't entirely fair. She had put her own life on the line, and was still doing it, if present circumstances counted. But that was before she found out she was pregnant.

That had changed everything. The moment the doctor had come into her hospital room, beaming with the news, her entire life had crowded around her as if a plastic snow dome had been clamped around it. And she hadn't particularly liked what she saw. Through the eyes of an expectant mother, she viewed herself as a girl, tugging off her hair bow and all the ruffles on her dress and tossing them into the trash the first day of school. As a teenager, making every school team—including football—just to get a rise out of her mother. As an adult, seeking every thrill and adventure she could.

Her mother's face had loomed, superimposed, yes, pinched with disapproval, but also etched with worry. In that moment she realized she had another life to consider now. She also understood that she would always worry her mother. The condition went hand-in-hand with motherhood.

But she couldn't help thinking that if her father had been alive, if he had played a role in their lives, the load would have been easier for all of them.

Melanie rolled over and pressed her face into the pillow. The insight had not come easily. After she had been released from the hospital and was at home, sitting in a daze in the back yard, and Craig had proposed—she had accepted.

A proposal it was important for her now to reject. For both their sakes. And she owed it to him to discuss it face-to-face before telling anyone else.

She sat and let her gaze wander around the room. There was something comforting about being in Marc's room. She got up and ran a hand over a poster of a race car. The tape had come off the bottom right corner. Looking closer, she rolled it up a bit. No, it couldn't be....

It wasn't difficult to loosen the yellow tape on the left corner. She rolled up the poster to confirm her suspicions. Grimacing, she stared at the definitive pinup poster. Farrah Fawcett. Well, that explained some things. Like why Marc was so obsessed with her breasts. Gad, this poster had to be...

She looked at the flip hairstyle even she had emulated, not wanting to think about the time or the fact that she could remember it.

She sighed and tried to smooth the race car poster. It immediately rolled halfway up. Didn't these people ever paint?

She smiled, counting all the things she had learned about Marc in the past twenty-four hours. His reluctant capacity for deep emotion. She pulled on her jeans, leaving on the faded Redskins T-shirt Marc had given her to wear. His close bond with his brothers. She slipped into her new athletic shoes. The tragedy in his past that had taken the only female influences from his life.

Biting solidly on her bottom lip, she tried to ignore the things that came together in her mind. The poster that told her Marc held on tightly to the past. His cautious admission that he was afraid he'd never see her again.

The only problem was the realization came about three months too late.

She quickly made up the bed, then left the room and all its puzzles behind, descended the stairs and moved toward the side door. She hadn't seen Marc, but she guessed he was probably outside watching the place. Which was just as well. Right now she really needed to talk to Sean.

She was glad to find him in the kitchen, nursing a cup of coffee.

"Morning. Sleep well?"

Melanie's face heated, remembering she hadn't done much sleeping. "Great. I slept great." She cleared her throat. "That coffee fresh?"

"It's drinkable."

She absently mimicked David's movements from the night before, taking a mug from the cupboard and pouring herself a half cup of the hot java. A couple of sips couldn't hurt.

Sean took the cup from her hands and dumped the contents down the drain before she could open her mouth. "Jake dug out some decaffeinated something or other for you. Here it is." He picked up a red-and-white box. "Tea."

Melanie grimaced. "I'd much rather have the coffee."

Sean filled the teapot, his actions his only response.

Resigned, she sat at the table and pulled the crossword he'd been working on her way.

"Hungry? Mitch read over the nutritional information on all of the cereal boxes and said this had the most vitamins." Sean nudged a box in her direction.

She laughed. "That's the first time I've heard someone call sugar-coated cereal nutritious."

David stumbled into the room, his jeans slung low on his hips, shirtless, his hair sticking up at all angles. "I thought I heard you." He reached into a cupboard and produced a banana. "Here. I saved this for you."

Melanie shook her head in disbelief. She'd thought Marc was a handful. Five more of him was too much.

Still, it was much easier to accept the banana, pour the cereal into the bowl he handed her and allow Sean to pour some milk than it was to argue.

Sean frowned at his youngest son. "David, don't you think it would be a good idea to put some clothes on, what with a guest in the house and all?"

David glanced at himself, seemingly unaffected by his half-dressed appearance. She guessed she was lucky he hadn't wandered in in his boxer shorts. She shook her head again, the origins of Marc's behavior becoming less and less a mystery. *It must be genetic.*

David shrugged, then stumbled out of the room, leaving her and Sean alone.

Melanie crunched on the cereal. "Sean," she said tentatively between bites. "Do you remember what you said to me in the hospital?"

She watched him stiffen. He faced the stove, apparently watching the kettle. "Depends on what you're referring to."

Melanie shifted, uneasy. "About my deciding to keep the baby?"

He slowly turned in her direction, his blue eyes serious beneath his bushy salt-and-pepper eyebrows. "What, that I thought it was a good idea if you got married?"

She nodded, remembering she hadn't thought the advice outdated coming from him. He had seemed genuinely concerned about her raising a child on her own. Which was funny, because she would have suspected a conspiracy had her mother broached the subject. "You meant that I should marry Marc, didn't you?"

He was quiet for a moment before he said, "At first I did. I'd never seen my boy as worked up as he was while you were lying in that hospital. He hounded me night and day until I agreed to go in there, you know, on the sly."

His expression grew serious. "But the more I got to know you, and, well, after I met that Craig fellow…"

Melanie stared into her cereal bowl, remembering when Craig had come to visit while she was talking to Sean.

"And he appeared like a decent enough sort. Well, I thought that you were the better one to make the decision about who you should spend the rest of your life with."

He coughed. "You know, who should play the role as father of your baby."

She squinted at him. "But you're the baby's grandfather."

Sean turned as the kettle began to whistle. "My first. I know." He took the kettle from the burner but didn't make a move to fill the mug sitting on the counter. "Hell, Mellie, I didn't do a very good job bringing my own boys up. I didn't have any right telling you what you should do with your own child." Silence reigned as he finally poured the water to let the tea steep. "I will say I'm awfully glad Marc knows about the child and that I'll now get that chance to play granddaddy." He smiled at her sadly. "That is, if you'll let me."

"Of course I'll let you," Melanie whispered, her throat clogged with tears.

She took her bowl to the sink, rinsed it and put it in the dishwasher. She joined Sean at the table. They sat across from each other.

"Sean?"

He lifted his gaze to hers.

"Thanks." She gestured absently with her hands. "Not just for now. But for…well, for being there when I was in the hospital."

She saw a depth of emotion in his eyes that made her chest tighten. A curiously familiar expression she swore she'd seen in Marc's eyes. "Anytime, Mellie. Anytime."

12

MARC SPOTTED MEL the instant she opened the door. His heart did a funny little thing in his chest just seeing her coming from the house he'd grown up in. She even caught the door before it could slam, as though she'd been doing it for years.

He kicked the back of his boot against the large rock he sat on, wanting to call out to her but not sure if he should. While she slept last night, nestled safe and warm in his arms, he'd been wide-awake, mulling over everything.

He watched her run a hand over her belly, appearing completely oblivious that she did it. He experienced a mixed burst of pride and fear and forced himself to swallow a huge dose of reality.

She doesn't want you, sport.

He looked around. The grass was overgrown, trampled beneath his and his brothers' footsteps. He rubbed the back of his neck. The trouble was, he really couldn't blame Mel for not wanting to marry him. The minute he'd learned about the baby, nearly the first words out of his mouth were, "You're marrying me." No romantic proposal, no declarations of love.

Love.

There was that word again.

He grimaced. What in the hell did he know about love? Sure, he supposed he loved his family. But Mel? She walked to the front of the house, away from him. He did know that the first few days she'd been in that hospital he'd hurt like hell. And that when he'd thought he'd lost her... Well, the ring was still burning a hole in his pocket.

He knew why he'd bought that engagement ring, but he didn't really know *why*. He'd told himself it was because it was what Mel had wanted. But not even that excuse held water anymore. Not when he remembered how nervous he'd been when he'd decided on the ring because it matched the color of her eyes. Not when he'd felt both proud and scared to death when he'd stood outside the hospital, then later, outside her mother's house, all decked out in a suit, ready to propose to her, only to discover she was marrying someone else.

But did he *love* her?

He bit off a curse. Mel at least deserved someone who knew what love was and knew how to show it.

And his son? Or daughter, he quickly reminded himself. What did he or she deserve?

"Someone who knows how to be a parent," he said quietly.

Truth be told, along with the excitement he felt about becoming a father, he was also more scared than he'd ever been in his life.

Mel turned in his direction, apparently having heard him. He rubbed his face and looked at his watch. David should be taking over soon. He needed the break. While it was part of his job to go for long stretches on watch, the way his mind had been working overtime…well, he could use a good, long shower and a couple cups of coffee.

"Here."

He looked up to find Mel standing directly in front of him, holding out a cup of what he'd just been dreaming about. He mumbled his thanks and took a long sip. He tried to hand it back.

"I can't have it, remember?" she said with a small smile. "Anyway, you look like you need it more than I do."

"Gee, thanks."

She sat down on the rock next to him. "You're welcome."

He scanned her profile, thinking she appeared as sober as he felt. Obviously she'd been doing some thinking of her own.

"Well," he murmured.

She gave him a weak smile.

A few minutes had passed in silence before she said, "I saw the poster of your old girlfriend on your wall."

He squinted against the rising sun. "Huh?"

She looked at him for the first time since sitting down. "Farrah?"

He continued to frown until he registered what she was saying. "Oh." He cleared his throat. "Unfortunately I had to share her with the entire male population." *Just like I'm going to have to share you with one male in particular.*

The thought came out of nowhere.

"I wanted to tell you that I…understand about your past," she said.

He scanned her face. What did a picture of a woman in a swimsuit have to do with his past? He grimaced and shook his head. He didn't get it.

And that was just the point. He would never understand how her mind worked. No matter how many women's magazines and relationship books he read, none of it would help him when it came to Mel. "Connect to your feminine side," one of the books had encouraged. He bit back a curse, finally admitting he might not have one of those. The stupid thing was, he wasn't sure if he was upset about that—or relieved.

He and Mel existed on two separate planes, their differences outnumbering their similarities. That had bothered him since the beginning. It might very well be what made him hang back when she had sought a closer connection.

He rubbed his palm against the rough denim of his jeans. "You'd better go inside. I don't want you to catch a chill."

"I can take care of myself."

He sighed. "Let me rephrase that. My watch is over, all right? I'm going inside. Would you like to come, or do you want to stay out here?"

She lifted her chin. "I think I'll sit out here awhile longer."

Marc shrugged, pretending he didn't care. "Have it your way."

He began to get up, then sat down. "By the way, I think you're right. You shouldn't marry me. In fact, I think it's a pretty good idea if you go ahead and marry Craig."

MELANIE SAT in stunned silence, watching Marc squirm next to her.

"I'm sorry, I didn't mean for it to come out quite that way," he said, looking torn. He cleared his throat and met her gaze head-on. "You said you loved Craig. And I'm sure he loves you. And the baby... Well, I can still play a role in his life, can't I?"

Melanie's mind refused to register what he was saying. "Look, Marc—"

He shook his head. "It's okay. You don't have to do any more explaining. Your reasons for not marrying me have finally settled in. I won't be bothering you anymore." He rose from the rock and started walking toward the house.

Melanie finally convinced herself she wasn't hearing things and leaped up.

"What?" she asked, hurrying after him. "What did you just say?"

She reached him and nearly ran right into him. "You can't just say something like that, then walk away! I want an explanation."

She would have thought he looked altogether too cute, too tortured. If only she wasn't feeling as if he'd ripped her heart out.

"What's there left to explain, Mel? You love Craig. I'm assuming he loves you. I don't want to stand in the way of your happiness. It was wrong of me to do so to begin with."

She didn't know whether she wanted to hit him or burst out crying.

The sound of a car engine broke the early morning silence. It took a second for her to recognize it. By the time she did, Marc had pulled the gun from the waist of her jeans and was hustling her toward the house.

"Get inside."

"I'm not—"

"Come on, Mel, now is not the time for an argument."

Her gaze flicked toward the approaching car. It looked familiar, but she couldn't be sure from this distance. The door opened, and Sean pulled her inside just as David and a half-dressed Mitch came thundering into the kitchen.

Melanie's heart beat double time. She looked down, realizing Marc had taken her gun. Her hands rested solidly against her belly, as though protecting the child there.

She caught Sean's expression. Emotions Melanie could recognize swept through the older man's eyes. Joy, sorrow, undiluted fear for her and his grandchild. Had he heard the exchange between her and Marc? Did he know Marc had told her to marry another man?

The moment was broken when Jake ran by, buttoning a shirt over his unfastened slacks. Melanie stared, dumbfounded by how quickly they got going. Sure, they were all in law enforcement, but these McCoys... As witless as they appeared on a personal level, they were like a well-tuned military unit used to dealing with situations like this. She shuddered, wondering if that could be the case.

No...

"Oh, no, you don't, Mellie." Sean blocked her way when she was ready to bolt out the door. "You're going to stay inside and keep yourself and my grandchild safe."

For the second time that morning, Melanie felt her face

go hot. If the command had come from Marc, she would have fought him. But his father she couldn't refuse.

"Do you really think it's Hooker?" she asked.

He frowned. "I don't know, but I suspect the boys will find out soon enough."

She nodded and stayed in the living room. For the sake of her baby.

She sank into the recliner and rested her head in her hands. She pondered exactly how she had gotten into this mess and whether or not anything would ever be the same again.

She started to get up to look through the front window when an arm snaked around her from behind, pinning her to the chair.

"Don't move," a male voice warned.

Oh, God.

Cold fear ran straight through Melanie, paralyzing her as much as the command. It had to be Hooker.

Her mind raced crazily. How did he get in? She flashed to that morning, when she'd found the house stuffy and had rebelliously opened a window Marc had locked. She smelled the fresh Virginia air on Hooker's clothes. He had likely just gained access, which meant he'd likely come in while she had been talking to Marc.

She closed her eyes. If anything proved her decision to resign her position with the secret service had been right, her actions that morning did. She'd allowed emotion and just plain insolence to interfere with the protection against a serious threat, undermining the actions of those who had sworn to help her. Every one of the McCoy brothers was even now swooping down on what might be an innocent visitor, while she had not only let Hooker into the house…she was utterly alone with him.

Her throat tightening, Melanie reached for a gun that was no longer there.

"Stay quiet." Her assailant released his grasp and rounded the chair. Melanie's stomach hurt so much she thought she might experience her first bout of morning sickness.

"Hooker," she whispered.

"This isn't exactly the way I planned things, Mel. You have to understand that." He appeared nervous. Melanie knew from training and experience that a panicky man was the most dangerous one. He was more apt to act out of fear than to think things through. Her gaze was glued to the gun in his shaking hands.

"I tried calling you. Why didn't you take my calls? Why wouldn't you listen to me, Mel?"

She looked him full in the face. "All the talking's been done, Hooker."

"No!" He pointed the gun at her. "You've got to listen to me!"

Melanie tried to make herself one with the chair upholstery, hardly daring to breathe. *Keep your eyes raised. The hardest thing to do is to shoot someone while looking into their eyes.* The snippet from her training did nothing to make her feel better.

"I mean, no," he said a little more calmly. "Not nearly enough's been said. You need to know the truth. I'm here to tell you what really went down that night." He swiped at the sweat on his forehead with the cuff of his denim shirt, a shirt Melanie knew he'd stolen from a clothesline. "I asked...demanded to talk to you after everything went down, but you...you'd been shot. They wouldn't let me explain things." His eyes held a desperate, crazy pleading. "You're the only one who can help me, Mel."

Melanie felt the ridiculous urge to cry. For the second time in as many days, she appreciated the irony of her predicament and hated it. She couldn't be more than fifty yards away from five prime, well-trained males, and she'd entered the only unsafe place on the property.

Hooker's hands shook so violently, she was afraid he would accidentally trip the trigger.

Keep it together, Mel. Keep it together.

"You don't understand. I didn't do it. It wasn't me, Mel. It wasn't me."

She attempted to push a response from her throat. "Then why have you been trying to kill me?"

"Kill you?" He stumbled back a couple of steps. "I haven't been trying to kill you. I've been trying to talk to you. Why…why would I want to kill you? I've been trying to save my ass." There was the sound of slamming car doors. Hooker jerked his head to listen, his anxiety quotient nudging up even further. "You're confusing me. I need to get this out, don't you see?"

There it was. The stillness she needed settled over her as a rare opportunity gaped wide-open.

Hooker continued. "That night… It's kind of like a blur to me, you know? One minute I'm checking out a suspicious noise, the next I'm waking up on the cold ground with your boyfriend's knee in my chest." His voice rose in pitch as he continued. "Don't you see? It wasn't me, Mel. It was—"

Vaulting from the chair, Melanie acted on pure instinct. With her right hand, she forced the barrel of the gun away while she slipped her left leg behind his right knee and pushed against his shoulder. As he fell, she tugged the gun out of his grip, then planted her foot solidly against his solar plexus, pinning him to the floor.

She locked the safety on the gun, then allowed herself a moment to enjoy the afterglow. Oh, yes, she still had it.

Hooker started to struggle. Afraid he might get loose, she started to pull her hand back, the weight of the gun she held promising more strength to the impending blow.

"Damn it, it wasn't me!" Tom Hooker flinched. "It was Roger!"

Her hand connected with the side of his head just as his words slipped through the protective adrenaline haze clouding her thoughts.

MELANIE'S MIND reeled as she stared at the unconscious man she had slowly, methodically bound with curtain ties. Hooker's last words echoed as if he were saying them over and over.

It was Roger.... It was Roger.... It was Roger....

After three months of replaying the memories from that night, of reliving the horrifying moments in her sleep, feeling as if there was something she was missing, something that didn't ring true, she knew the reason. That shadowy figure she had caught trying to slip through the senator's window, the faceless man who had shot her hadn't been Hooker. It had been his partner, Roger Westfield.

A man now Marc's partner.

Facts that supported Hooker's claim accumulated in her mind. Hooker's repeated attempts to contact her. His unwavering proclamation of innocence. The staff psychologist saying the recurring nightmares were trying to tell her something. Marc telling her during the drive to the safe house that he would never have thought Hooker capable of doing what they all thought he had done.

"Yoo-hoo, Melanie. Are you in here, dear?" A pause, then, "Let go, you wicked creature!"

Melanie's heart dropped somewhere down around her ankles as she heard her mother's voice from the kitchen. Caught somewhere between shock that she could have been so wrong and alarm that the man responsible for almost taking her life was still out there somewhere, she absently checked the tie around Hooker's feet, then haltingly stepped toward the other room. Just short of the door, she stopped, gathering her wits. Despite everything that had just happened, she realized a new fear. The fear that her mother would instantly know what had happened between her and Marc the past two days. As sure as if Melanie had a scorecard taped to the front of her T-shirt.

"Melanie Marie, where— Oh, there you are, dear."

Melanie stepped into the kitchen to find the cramped

quarters solidly divided into two camps. The McCoys stood beside her or behind her—large, hulking men who made her feel slightly intimidated but also as though she had the power of God on her side.

On the other side of the kitchen was her mother along with two state police patrolmen and...Craig.

Melanie's heart skipped a beat, and her skin burned with guilt. But there was no anger in Craig's eyes. Instead she watched worry turn into obvious relief, then curiosity as he eyed her disheveled appearance, then looked at Marc. When he gave her a small smile, relief washed through Melanie's tense muscles. She knew without asking that she hadn't lost her best friend.

Her gaze shifted to a movement closer to the floor.

Oh, God.

Goliath.

Her mother had taken a time-out when Melanie had entered, but now returned to the losing end of a game of tug-of-war with Mitch's Saint Bernard, Goliath. Melanie rushed forward, realizing it was her bridal bouquet that was locked in Goliath's jaws. White lily petals sprang from the arrangement like mammoth snowflakes, covering the tile and her mother's pink shoes.

Craig tried to distract the dog as Wilhemenia yelped for someone to help. Then she lost her grip. Before Melanie could do anything, the hulking hound of a dog galloped from the room, triumphant.

There were several undisguised snickers from behind Melanie as her mother finally turned toward her, her face red, her hair sticking out from her usual smooth chignon. "Melanie, I want you to explain to me this minute what's going on."

"I—"

"For three days I've been worrying myself to death over your well-being—"

"Mom—"

"Ever since this twit—" she waved impatiently in

Marc's direction but seemed to have a problem isolating exactly which one he was "—kidnapped you from the powder room."

"He's not—"

"Then yesterday morning you call, trying to tell me something—" Melanie rolled her eyes, remembering she hadn't been able to get a word in edgewise "—and I nearly go deaf from this horrible sound, and the line goes dead."

"That's because—"

"Poor Craig has been as worried as I have. He's not left my side, or Joanie's, once throughout this entire ordeal. Except to go do what nature intended, of course, but that's excusable considering all the coffee he's—"

Craig gave Melanie an understanding look then touched her mother's arm in an obvious effort to stop her. "I think she gets the picture, Mrs. Weber."

"Then we pull up here and that overgrown creature—"

"Mother!"

Wilhemenia gave Melanie a reprimanding look. "You're right to raise your voice to me. Here I am chattering away when we should be seeing to unfinished business. Officers, arrest that man." She gestured toward where she thought Marc stood, but instead pointed to Jake. She started to tuck her hair into place. "And I think you should be able to work up something by way of accessories with the—" she faltered as she looked over the McCoy bunch "—rest of them."

"Over my dead body will you touch any of my boys," Sean said, his voice booming commandingly through the room.

Wilhemenia fell silent. *Silent.* Melanie stared at her. She'd never seen anyone capable of quelling her mother's incessant tongue. Lord knew *she* was incapable of it.

She looked between Sean and her mother, both powerful personalities. She recalled that every time Sean had come into her hospital room, her mother had made herself instantly scarce.

Craig seemed to notice the odd reaction and raised an eyebrow at Melanie.

Wilhemenia finally regained her voice, though it was noticeably softer, more self-conscious. "Your wedding is in three hours, Melanie. I think—"

"Until Hooker is caught, Melanie isn't going anywhere," Marc said, stepping next to Melanie and crossing his arms.

She wanted to scream as she watched Marc size up Craig. That's all she needed. For Marc to coldcock her best friend because, like her mother, he didn't understand that there wouldn't be a wedding. She wasn't going to marry Craig. Craig knew that without her having to say a word. The only reason he had proposed to begin with was that she'd been convinced Marc wasn't going to play a role in her baby's life. One look had told Craig that all that had changed.

She stared at Marc, exasperated. Why couldn't he be more observant? Or was he acting on emotion, as she had that morning when she opened the window?

She raised her voice. "Will everyone just shut up a minute and let me speak?"

The room went suddenly, blessedly quiet.

Melanie tried to figure out where to start. She looked at her mother first.

"Mom, I'm sorry you had to worry about me, but there isn't going to be any arresting here. Not of Marc or any of his brothers." Wilhemenia opened her mouth to speak, but Mel hurried on. "While I didn't agree at the time, Marc took me because the man who shot me three months ago had escaped from prison. So he did what he did to protect me. It was the right thing, the only thing to do."

She glanced at Marc, remembering his cryptic words earlier when he told her she should marry Craig. She looked at him, wishing they could have finished that conversation. She knew there wasn't going to be a wedding. But after what he'd said, should she tell him that?

"As for Hooker," she said quietly, "while all of you were outside protecting me from my mother and my…fiancé—" she had to push the last word out "—Hooker was already in the house." She took some pleasure in their dumbfounded expressions. "He's tied up in the living room."

"What?" Marc asked as his brothers bolted into the next room.

She nodded. Normally, she might have enjoyed a moment like this, proving she could still hold her own under fire, but she couldn't. Not knowing what she did. Not knowing that Hooker hadn't been the one who shot her. And especially since she'd knocked Hooker out for all his efforts.

"So," she said, wanting to deal with Marc and the sticky situation she found herself in the middle of before telling him his new partner was the real shooter.

"I still think—"

"Keep out of this, Mother," Melanie said.

Shocked by the firm order, her mother opened and closed her mouth several times, reminding Melanie of a hooked bass.

"Did you mean what you said this morning?" she quietly asked Marc. "You know, about my marrying…"

Her heart contracted in her chest. She waited for his response, some sign, a flicker in his expression, but there was none. And he was taking far too long to respond.

If ever she needed Marc to speak his mind, it was now.

Her mother touched her arm. "Melanie, dear, I really hate to interrupt—"

"I thought it was your life's occupation." Her mother looked as if she'd been slapped. Melanie cringed. "Sorry, that was uncalled for."

"I meant every word," Marc said, his expression stony. "I wish you and Craig every happiness."

Melanie would have whacked him if only her heart weren't cracking in half. "That makes two of us. Only there isn't going to be a wedding. Craig and I are not getting married."

Marc and Wilhemenia stared at her as if she'd lost the last of her marbles while Craig slipped his arm around her shoulders, supporting her every step of the way. A move she was thankful for, because she was going to need his friendship to see her through this.

She cleared the tears from her throat. "But that's not all. The man tied up in the room next door is not the one we should be looking for. The man who shot me is Roger Westfield."

13

SHELL-SHOCKED. That's the best way Melanie could describe how she felt. After all that had happened, it felt really weird sitting in the church antechamber pretending to get ready for her wedding. It seemed a shameful waste, really, seeing as she had planned everything out. Well, Joanie had planned everything out, and she had agreed, right down to the little nosegays the bridesmaids were going to wear, and the rosebuds being passed out instead of rice to toss at her, and...her groom.

Problem was, she didn't have a groom. And she probably never would.

Craig.

At least she still had her best friend. He really didn't know what to make of what was going on between her and Marc. *She* didn't know what to make of it, for that matter. One minute they were having the most incredibly touching sex of her life; the next he was telling her, no, *ordering* her to marry Craig. It didn't make any sense. None at all.

But Craig didn't need it to make sense. Yes, he'd told her during the long drive home, he was a little disappointed.

"I wouldn't be human if I didn't admit that my pride has taken a hell of a blow," he said, getting a hug for his admission, although not the type of hug Mel shared with Marc. The affection she traded with Craig was of a brotherly nature, and could never have been anything more, she realized. "I'd also be lying if I didn't say I'm relieved." He'd smiled at her. "I love you, Melanie, but..."

"Not in *that* way," she had finished for him. "I love you the same way, Pookems."

She only wished her feelings for Marc were as easy to sort through and settle.

She was coming to expect that from her relationship with Marc McCoy. Her heart gave a painful squeeze. From here on out, he'd play a role in her life, but only that of her child's father, not her lover or anything more.

There was a brief knock at the door. Quickly sitting up, she rubbed her cheeks to put some color into them.

"Yoo-hoo," her mother called out as she opened the door.

Melanie made an effort not to slouch.

Wilhemenia quietly closed the door.

"How is everything?" she asked, coming to stand behind her daughter.

Terrible. Awful. I want to crawl into bed and cry for a month. "Fine."

Wilhemenia fluffed the back of her hair, then rested her hand on Melanie's shoulder. "You look beautiful."

Melanie blinked at her in the mirror. Had she heard right? Had her mother just given her a compliment? No, it wasn't possible. Especially not when all of Wilhemenia's carefully approved plans had been ruined. Besides, there was always something wrong, some different way she could have done her hair, an alternate color of lipstick or at least a reprimand about her poor posture. "Excuse me?" she heard herself say.

Wilhemenia smiled. "I said you're beautiful." Her gaze faltered, and she began toying with the sleeves of Melanie's dress. "I know I probably haven't told you that nearly enough, but I've always thought it." She paused. "I just wished your life could have turned out different from mine."

Melanie's dress rustled as she turned to face her.

Certainly her mother wasn't telling her what she thought she was? It couldn't be possible. Had Wilhemenia been pregnant when she married? Her face went hot. She reminded herself that her mother didn't know of her condition. She peered at her a little more closely. Or did she?

"Are you trying to tell me something, Mother?"

Wilhemenia pulled a chair from the corner. She *pulled* it. She didn't pick it up and carefully move it. She hung her purse on the chair, then sank into it. But she still didn't say anything.

"Mom?"

"Do you remember what you asked me?"

Melanie watched her take papers from the cavernous depths of her purse.

"You know, in the bathroom, during the rehearsal dinner?" She avoided Melanie's gaze as she put the papers in her hands. "It's difficult to believe that was just three days ago. It seems like a lifetime."

You can say that again. Melanie smiled to hide her thoughts. "Sorry, I don't. Remember what I asked you, that is."

Wilhemenia cleared her throat, an odd sound considering how elegant she usually was. "You, um, asked if I had loved your father."

Melanie stared. Her mother stroked her hand. "I remember now."

"The truth is, yes, I did love your father. More than life itself."

Melanie looked at her. In the years since her father died, her mother had if not quietly cursed her father, at least blamed him for leaving her with two girls to raise. Melanie realized she had never tried to look into her mother's heart for the truth. She'd merely accepted it, and yes, even judged her on it.

Her mother stared at the ceiling. "Yes, I know you're pregnant, Melanie." Her gaze shifted. "I overheard the day you told…well, when you told Sean about it." Color touched her cheeks. Melanie guessed it was because of embarrassment. "I was coming back from the nurse's station and saw him sitting with you, as he often did. I didn't want to interrupt, but…" She trailed off and gave a guilty little smile. "But that's not what this is about."

"You were pregnant, too, weren't you? When you and Dad married?"

Her mother nodded. "Not that anyone knew. I was very careful about keeping it a secret. In those days when a young woman was single and pregnant in a small town, it was more than scandalous, it was…" She laughed weakly. "Talk about taking the long way around the bush. I'm just going on, aren't I?"

Melanie peered at her closely. She had always thought her mother rambled on because she wanted, required command of the conversation. She'd never thought for a minute that she chattered because she was nervous.

"Anyway," Wilhemenia said, "I think you ought to know I always considered you my miracle disguised as an accident."

Melanie's throat thickened. So much was shifting into focus.

"And I did love your father. I did. But I was miserable. I let that love get in the way of a happy marriage. Nothing was ever enough. He didn't do things the right way. He must not have loved me as much as I loved him. The list was endless. And when he died, I was so angry at him because I thought he had failed me in the ultimate way. He hadn't loved me enough to fight to stay with me."

Melanie shifted, unsure what to do, what to say. She'd never shared confidences with her mother.

Wilhemenia gave a quiet, humorless laugh. "There I go again." She cleared her throat and gazed directly into Melanie's eyes. "What I'm trying to say here is that I saw you heading down that same path with Marc. And I had to…I had to intervene."

Melanie let the words sink in. "Are you telling me what I think you are? That you…" *What? Chased big Marc Mc-*

Coy away? Sent him packing? "You orchestrated our breakup?"

Wilhemenia patted her hand. "I didn't have to orchestrate anything, Melanie. It was happening all by itself. I merely stepped up the beat a little."

Melanie got up from the chair. "I can't believe you did that." She paced across the room. The references Marc had made about her mother not passing on messages, turning him away when she was recovering... She hadn't believed him. She'd thought her mother had no reason to want them apart. True, Wilhemenia had never liked Marc, but she had never meddled in Melanie's life to that extent before. Now she saw her mother had the most potent reason there was—she'd wanted to protect her daughter from suffering the same heartache she had suffered.

The reason, combined with Wilhemenia's tenacity, explained a lot but changed little. Not now. The sad truth was that what her mother said made a lot of sense. She stopped pacing and stared at the papers in her hands. *They were all notes from Marc.*

But she had been willing to settle for a loveless marriage with Craig. Well, not completely loveless. They had the bond created from lifelong friendship.

But marriage to Marc would be torture. Her love for him—without his love in return—would be the destructive, passionate, demanding type. That was the threat and always had been.

"I think I'd better go join everyone in the back of the chapel before Marc comes and pulls me out," her mother said quietly. "I'm sorry, Melanie. I...I just wanted to let you know that."

Melanie nodded, worrying her bottom lip between her teeth.

She sank into the chair in front of the mirror, not really seeing her reflection, her thoughts jumbled. She stared at the papers in her hands, then shoved them into her purse.

It didn't matter anymore, did it? It didn't matter that her mother had played a role in securing her and Marc's breakup. That there were reasons behind Marc's absence at the hospital. None of it mattered because she and Marc just weren't meant to be.

There was another knock at the door. Melanie blinked back stinging tears. When Craig walked in, she blurted, "I love him, Craig."

MARC SAT in the back of the nondescript van, oblivious to the heat as he stared at the chapel across the street. Bedford. The small town was neat and manicured and seemed to demand, "Do not enter unless you, too, are equally orderly." Not for the first time, he found it odd that a product of a place like this—much less a woman— had run off and joined the secret service. He grimaced and absently rubbed the back of his neck. Then again, Mel didn't live to satisfy anyone's expectations.

Just when he thought he had it all figured out, she changed all the rules. She wasn't marrying Craig. A part of him was relieved. A greater part ached because she wasn't marrying him, either.

He recognized a late-arriving guest as the uncle he'd encountered outside the men's room at the rehearsal dinner. He spoke into the two-way radio and asked the plain-clothes officer just inside the chapel door to escort him to where all the other guests were, to the pastor's quarters in the back. Considering the time element and the need for everything to look normal, he and Mel had decided the ceremony should appear to go ahead as planned. Even the guests didn't know why they had to wait in the back rather than take a seat in one of the pews. It hadn't been easy, but he and his brothers had called in favors from every law enforcement official they knew to fill those same pews with fake guests. Every guest in that chapel was armed to the teeth and ready to take out the shooter within the blink of an eye.

"You're nuts, you know?"

Marc was so engrossed in trying to catch a glimpse of Mel, he had forgotten Mitch was in the van with him, along with two surveillance experts. "To keep you out of trouble," Mitch had said after he and Mel had questioned a barely conscious Tom Hooker, then put together what looked like the last of their plans.

Hooker had been hauled off by the state police. A hearing was already scheduled for first thing Monday morning. Mel had taken off with Craig and her mother, and Marc had sat at the kitchen table making phone calls, his four brothers and his father staring at him and shaking their heads while Brando meowed piteously at his feet.

"What?" he'd said after the stare fest had gone on a minute too long.

"You picked a hell of a time to lose the good sense God gave you, Marc," his father had said. "That girl is family."

"What would you have me do? Trade places with her last groom?"

Their silence told him all he needed to know. And he'd answered them with a series of choice curse words that raised even his father's eyebrows.

Marc grumbled, earning a chuckle from Mitch. "You know, there's something bothering me about this whole thing," Marc said under his breath.

Mitch took a long swig of coffee and glanced at his watch. "Yeah, I'd say having your woman the target of an assassin is cause for bother."

Marc glowered at him. "Not that. Well, yeah, that, too, but there's something else."

Mitch stretched over one of the bucket seats and turned the ignition key. The van roared to life. He turned the air conditioner on full blast. One of the other men thanked him. "What is it?"

"I don't know. I keep thinking I should have known." He remembered going into the other room to find Hooker as good as hog-tied. Pride had filled him to know Mel had done that. Sorrow had also pierced him. She could take care of herself. Pregnant, single or any other way.

Marc caught sight of a girl of around six in a pink frilly dress hurrying up the chapel steps, her skirt blowing around thin legs. His throat grew tight as he watched her and her father being ushered inside by the undercover officer. In so many years he might find himself with a little girl like that. Or a boy. What would it be like to be a father? Not just a part-time dad, but a real, honest-to-goodness dad? Despite the cool air circulating through the van, he broke out in a sweat.

"You know, all along Hooker maintained his innocence."

"You can't blame yourself, Marc. You know what Pops always says."

"All guilty men plead innocent because they have nothing to lose." Marc rubbed his chin. "That's all well and good, but Pops was never in the academy with the one in question." He shook his head.

"And Bundy might be a senator by now, if not president, if he hadn't been caught. Come on, Marc, we both know appearances have nothing to do with it."

"Still, I should have known." Marc went silent. He thought about the tests that had been run on Hooker's service revolver. They had come up negative. He had dismissed it by saying Hooker had another gun and had disposed of it before he was caught. Only it wasn't Hooker's gun they should have been looking at, but Roger Westfield's.

If he had been wrong about Hooker, what else had he been wrong about?

"Damn." Marc jerked open the van door, causing the men inside to scramble for cover.

Mitch caught his sleeve. "Where are you going?"

"He's already in there."

14

MELANIE NODDED to the plainclothes officer keeping watch over the balcony entrance, then hurried up the stairs to watch the impostor bride walk down the aisle in a thick, gauzy veil. Clutching her revolver, she crouched a little lower behind the balcony railing in the back of the chapel, the sound of the organ at her elbow nearly deafening her. Her heart thudded dully in her chest as she methodically scanned the full pews below.

She didn't know how Marc had pulled all this off. Not able to pull in recognizable secret service agents, he'd relied instead on the vast network of law enforcement personnel available through his brothers and Sean. All the real guests—it had been too late to cancel the wedding, and besides, if they had, the setup might not have worked—had been safely and discreetly escorted to the pastor's private quarters at the back of the church, where, she was sure, they were all trying to figure out what was going on.

The bride finished the walk and stood next to a guy who looked an awful lot like Craig, but wasn't. Despite everything, Melanie fought back a smile. As far as brides went, this one—well, this one really took the cake.

The organist finally stopped playing and left the balcony, as instructed. Melanie backed up, hiding behind the large instrument, wishing she had had time to change out of the uncomfortable wedding dress she wore. But Joanie had been too intent on getting the stand-in's dress on, and her mother had been busily helping explain things to the real guests. In the chaos, Melanie couldn't even find her jeans.

It was probably for the best, because Marc hadn't wanted to let her out of his sight, and she wasn't about to tempt herself unnecessarily by undressing in front of him. No one knew as well as she did that nudity, specifically her own, and Marc were a lethal combination. She had a lot to work out, and she didn't need sex messing things up.

The fact remained that Marc had offered to marry her only for their child's sake, nothing more. Besides, he'd rescinded the offer that morning when he'd told her she should marry Craig.

She considered peering through the fan-shaped windows to look at the dark brown surveillance van parked on the street, but doing so would give her presence away. After a heated debate, it was decided that Marc shouldn't be seen anywhere near the chapel, in case Roger Westfield spotted him and figured out he was being set up. Melanie briefly closed her eyes. She only hoped they could get Westfield before he got them.

A rustling sounded behind her. Frowning, Melanie peered around the organ. Instead of the silver head of the organist, she saw a familiar dark one.

Roger.

Moving so he wouldn't spot her, Melanie slowly slid into the shadows, her palms growing instantly damp. *Not good.*

MARC RUSHED into the chapel, his breath coming in ragged gasps as he stuck to the shadows. He scanned the backs of the phony guests, making sure Roger hadn't somehow sneaked by, then turned to the door. The stand-in pastor's voice droned on, pretending to marry the couple down the aisle. Marc clutched his revolver close to his chest and wiped his forehead against his shoulder.

His instincts told him Roger was already here. So far

nothing had been said about Hooker's recapture, so the scumbag would think it was safe to continue his campaign to eliminate Mel and any possibility that she might remember what really happened three months ago. The idiot didn't know Mel had no idea Roger was the true shooter until two hours ago. Hell, neither had he, for that matter.

The best he could figure the situation after talking to Tom Hooker, the night of the assassination attempt it had been Roger, not Hooker, who had moved against the senator. Marc silently cursed, remembering his new partner's top-of-the-line sports cars and his many expensive outings.

He moved to the other side of the chapel.

Roger must have knocked Hooker out, and when Mel showed up, he shot her. Hooker had been already out of commission, coming to when gunshots were fired.

Marc wondered what it must have been like for Hooker to be fine one minute, then wake up on the ground the next with two agents on him—one of them his own partner—accused of attempting to assassinate the senator.

Running true to form in most assailant cases, when Hooker had tried to contact Mel to persuade her to listen to his pleas of innocence, she had refused to talk to him.

Then Roger's luck had run out. Four days ago Hooker had used his training to escape en route to his pretrial hearing and had managed to elude recapture. Marc grimaced. The guy had been good enough to get past him and his brothers, which was saying a whole hell of a lot. Only problem was, everyone knew he was heading for Mel. Which made Roger's plan pitifully simple: do away with Mel, and Hooker would take the fall for the crime forever.

Marc's chest tightened painfully. He only hoped Roger wasn't as good as Hooker.

His attention was pulled to the altar. From this distance, not even he could tell that the groom wasn't Craig and the bride wasn't Mel.

The stand-in pastor—who was a desk jockey ex-priest from his father's D.C. precinct—looked up and addressed the audience. "Speak now, or forever hold your peace."

Marc watched the groom hesitantly lift the bride's veil.

"Kiss me and you're dead meat," Jake said to the Craig look-alike.

His brother's threatening words made Marc wince. Not yet, you yo-yo. Westfield had to believe Jake in drag was Mel if they were to have a chance in hell of making this work.

He anxiously stepped forward, searching the guests again. He froze when he spotted Roger crouched behind the balcony railing, his rifle aimed straight at Jake.

Dear Lord, where's Mel?

"Yoo-hoo!" a familiar voice called a second before Mel's mother came in from the back. "I just thought you should know the natives are getting—"

"Hit the deck!" Marc shouted.

Jake tackled Mrs. Weber, covering her in wedding dress white, his cowboy boots peeking out from underneath as Marc aimed. The guests scrambled for cover, pulling out firearms, so the chapel was filled with the echoes of chambers loading, all of them looking for the unseen threat. Before Roger could squeeze off a shot, Mel appeared to his left. She whacked him in the arm with her revolver as he fired. The bullet harmlessly penetrated a plaster column.

Blood roaring in his ears, Marc thought about everything that had happened in the past three months. Mel being shot...finding out about her pregnancy...the recent attempts on her life. The revolver in his hands felt remarkably light, his focus on his target notably clear. He pulled off a shot, only at the last second lowering his aim.

Everything seemed to happen in slow motion. The bullet slammed against Roger's right shoulder. He dropped his rifle. It fell from the balcony to the marble tile near Marc's feet. Roger swayed, leaning precariously against the railing. Mel clutched him to prevent his fall, and Roger grabbed for her.

The railing creaked.

Marc's heart hiccuped in his chest.

Mel, no!

Then, suddenly, Roger was no longer against the railing, and Mel was carefully leaning over.

"Got him."

THERE WAS a certain surreal quality to the day, Marc thought, standing next to Mel on the chapel steps. For some odd reason, colors seemed brighter, the birds louder, and the air definitely smelled sweeter. And the decision he'd come to the instant he saw Mel was all right seemed all the more clear.

He moved out of the way as a paramedic hurried out and a federal criminalist headed in. Roger Westfield had been carted off on a stretcher, two marshals under the command of Connor and a pair of handcuffs guaranteeing he didn't have a chance to pass Go or collect $200.

When they'd wheeled him past, Roger had asked how he'd known he was the real shooter. Marc told him he'd be better off asking Tom Hooker that.

"Nice ceremony," Marc said to Mel as they waited, with the real and stand-in guests, for everything to be sorted out. Mel's relatives and neighbors buzzed with excitement, some of them still not completely grasping that there wasn't going to be a wedding, after all.

"I'd say it was memorable," Mel said quietly, giving him a broad smile.

Marc felt as if he'd been socked in the gut. "It'll be the talk of the town for, oh, I'd say well into the next generation."

Her expression told him she hadn't missed his reference to their baby. Their eyes met. No matter how hard he tried, Marc couldn't rip his gaze away from her. Lord help him, but he wanted to throw her over his shoulder and kidnap her all over again. And this time he'd do it right. Not because there was some madman out there who wanted to take her life. Not because she would be the mother of his child—children, he amended, suddenly deciding he wanted a horde of them. No, he wanted to handcuff her to him in more ways than one because he loved her more than anything else in this godforsaken world.

He loved her.

The realization surprised him in that it *didn't* surprise him.

His grin widened, and his heart skipped a few beats. Mel had always told him he was the last to catch on when it came to matters of the heart.

Jake walked by, Mrs. Weber lecturing him about a tear in the dress. Marc chuckled, then cleared his throat. "Do you think your guests are disappointed you and Craig aren't getting hitched?"

Mel eyed him closely. Her sexy green eyes shimmered in the midday sunlight. "Not too much, I don't think." She glanced at Craig, who stood with Joanie and his parents. "If there are a few, they'll forget all about it after the free food and drinks." She flashed him a smile. "Anyway, they got some great gossip."

Marc scanned her from forehead to chin. "So where does that leave you?"

She gazed toward the chapel doors and shrugged, looking particularly delectable in the dress she'd changed into at some point between Westfield's arrest and subsequent transport to the ambulance. Sure, maybe the hem was a little long and the shoes too flat, but the rich material hugged her in all the right places.

"I guess it makes me a single parent in the making," she answered.

"Yeah, me, too," he murmured. "Shame, seeing as we're so good together."

"I'm not marrying you, Marc."

He winced. "Ouch." He clasped his hands behind his back. "Why not?"

"You know why not."

"Because you think I only want to marry you because of the baby."

She looked at a nearby woman, who was craning to hear their conversation. She whispered, "Something like that."

"So live with me in sin, then."

To his surprise, she bellowed with laughter.

He shrugged. "Hey, I'll take it any way I can get it."

Mel started to walk away. Marc caught her arm. "Have I ever told you how much I love your smile?"

She hesitated. "No, I have to say that's a first." A wary shadow eclipsed her eyes. "I've never heard you utter the word love in relationship to anything."

He glanced down. "Anyway..."

She peered at him a little more closely.

"I guess the excitement's over, so I'll just be on my way."

He didn't miss the puzzled wrinkling of her forehead. Obviously she had expected more. "Okay." She started to turn away, then hesitated. "I'll keep you posted on how everything goes. You know, with the baby."

He gave her one of his biggest grins. "Oh, don't worry, Mel. I'll be in touch."

15

DESPITE HIS WORDS, Marc hadn't tried to contact her over the next two weeks.

Melanie sat on the front porch swing trying to catch a stray breeze while Joanie and her mother discussed catering menus inside. Brushing a strand of hair from her cheek, she thought it was funny how things could happen right under your nose without your being aware of it.

For the past twenty-five years Melanie, Joanie and Craig had been the terrific trio. And in all that time, she had never noticed that her sister and her best friend had secretly been in love with each other. She shook her head. If anything good had come out of the whole fiasco, it was the acknowledgment of that truth. While Marc had held her under lock and key, among other things—her cheeks burned with the memory—the mere act of being so close together for a prolonged period of time had created a veritable hothouse of romance for Craig and Joanie, as her mother told the story. Melanie smiled.

Hothouse of romance, indeed.

She rocked the swing and ran her hand over her belly. Overnight, it seemed, her stomach had gone from being flat to swelling into a noticeable mound. Joanie and Craig's impending wedding plans weren't the only good thing to come out of recent events, she amended. While in the days immediately following the "non-wedding of the century," as the townsfolk were referring to it, she had leaped on the phone every time it rang and had absently searched passing cars for signs of Marc, she had since found a certain, quiet peace. A peace that closely resembled the stillness she once felt as an agent. She'd come to terms with her impending single parenthood and knew that her baby would have all the love he would ever need right here with her, her mother, sister, and yes, even with Craig, in his role as uncle rather than father.

She'd started her new position as a security consultant at Beane and Sons and had begun mapping out plans for branching out on her own.

All in all, life was pretty good. Despite the bone-deep longing she often felt in the middle of the night.

If Marc wanted to play a role in their child's life—

Beneath her hand, she felt a nudge. Her breath catching, Melanie sat very still. That was very definitely a nudge.

She'd felt her baby move.

"Mellie?"

She glanced up to find Sean walking up the steps. She was so excited, she didn't stop to think it odd that he was there. She motioned him over.

"Come…sit down. I just felt the baby move for the first time."

Sean took the space next to her and hesitantly held his hand above her stomach. She smiled and pressed his fingers against the side of her belly.

They sat like that for a long moment. Melanie started to get discouraged. Maybe it hadn't been the baby, after all. Her doctor had said she should start to feel movement any day now, but—

"There!" she whispered in awe. "Did you feel it?"

Sean chuckled. A deep, proud sound that vibrated right through her. "I think you've got another McCoy male on your hands there, Mellie."

She glanced into his eyes. "Is something wrong? Is Marc all right?"

Sean smiled and hesitantly removed his hand from her stomach. "Marc's fine. As nervous as all get-out, but fine."

Melanie frowned. "Nervous? Why would he be nervous?"

"Hi, Mel."

She would recognize that sweet voice anywhere. A fascinating feeling not all that different from what she'd experienced when the baby moved spread through her as she turned her head.

There he was. Marc. In all his six-foot-two glory, grasping the porch column as if afraid to come up the steps.

Melanie didn't know if it was due to the pure delight she'd just experienced, but she didn't think he'd ever looked so boyishly handsome, so completely lovable.

She cleared her throat and quickly got up from the swing. Sean moved to help her, and she smiled at him. "I'm not at that point yet."

Sean scratched his head. "I hope you don't mind I came along for the visit, Melanie."

"No, no, of course not." She slid a quick glance in Marc's direction. He was standing in the same spot. All at once the peace she had found scattered, leaving her feeling confused and out of sorts. "Why don't you come in? I'll get you something to drink."

The screen door spring squeaked as she led the way in. She motioned for them to sit in the living room, then she hurried to the kitchen. She needed a few moments by herself to adjust to Marc's sudden appearance. She heard the crinkle of the plastic furniture covers as she started to step into the kitchen. She nearly hit her mother with the door.

There was Wilhemenia, a pitcher of lemonade and a couple of glasses already on a tray, along with a heaping plate of cookies.

Her mother smiled. "I've got it."

Melanie's heart skipped a beat as she realized her excuse for escape had been stolen from her. She briefly closed her eyes, then followed her mother into the living room.

"Melanie, dear, help me take this plastic off, won't you,

honey?'' Sean and Marc awkwardly got up and stood to the side as Wilhemenia started fussing with the cushions. ''You know we take this off when we're entertaining.''

Melanie's gaze locked onto Marc's, and they shared a small smile. Wilhemenia *never* took the plastic off her furniture, unless it was to change it.

''Of course,'' Melanie said. ''I don't know what I was thinking.''

After all the plastic was off and Melanie had taken it into the other room, she hesitantly settled into a chair, trying to figure out what Marc wanted. And why he hadn't come on his own.

One possibility struck her, and her gaze flew to his face. He didn't think she'd renege on her agreement to allow him to visit their baby, did he? Is that why he'd brought Sean along? To work out a more binding visitation agreement?

Wilhemenia kept up pleasant chatter, telling Sean all about the aftermath of Roger's capture and how she might have been shot herself if his son Jake hadn't saved her life. And didn't he have just a handsome bunch of boys, anyway.

Marc grinned at Mel, and she automatically smiled, feeling suddenly, oddly shy.

He motioned toward the front porch. ''Can I talk to you alone for a minute?''

She stared at him blankly. ''Um, sure.'' She got up. ''But why don't we go out back instead?'' She gave him a weak smile. ''I think we've already given the town enough to talk about.''

Wilhemenia and Sean didn't seem to notice their going as Sean started telling Melanie's mother about Mitch being left at the altar some years before. Melanie looked at Marc. He didn't appear to be tuned in to the conversation. In fact, he looked so nervous, he made her even more nervous.

She led the way to the back steps, then into the yard,

moving toward the gazebo. Only when Melanie started to enter did she realize how romantic the setting was. She stopped just outside the ivy-covered structure and looked at Marc expectantly, struggling to hold his gaze when just looking at him made her hurt all over.

He didn't say anything for a long moment as he shoved his hands into his jeans pockets. It was then Melanie realized he wore a yellow oxford shirt rather than his trademark black T-shirt, and nowhere to be seen was the ever-present vest he wore to hide his firearm.

Her gaze flicked to his face. "Marc, listen, I, um, just want you to know that I'll let you play as big or as little a role in our child's life as you want."

A half-smile turned up the corners of his lips. "That's what you think my being here is about?"

She looked toward the neighbor's. Mrs. Jennings was peering over the hedge she was trimming. "I didn't know, what with Sean being with you and all."

He chuckled quietly. "I brought Pops along because he wanted to come." He paused, and she returned her gaze to his face. "If I'd have known he could handle your mother that way, I would have brought him with me three months ago."

She frowned. *Three months ago?* What did he mean? She swallowed, realizing he must have meant when he tried to visit her, only to have her mother turn him away.

His gaze trailed to where her hands covered her stomach. He looked altogether awkward and irresistibly at odds with himself. "Is it true? Did you and Pops feel him move?"

Her answering smile was wide. "Or her," she reminded him. "Yes."

"Is he…or she still moving?"

Melanie's throat clogged with emotion. She wasn't sure if it was such a good idea to encourage Marc to touch her. "Would you like to feel it?"

Unlike Sean, Marc barely hesitated as he laid his hand

against her belly. She closed her eyes and guided his fingers to where she had felt the movement earlier. *Come on, baby, move for Daddy.*

As they stood there, birds rustling in the trees, the air carrying the keen scent of freshly mown grass, Melanie had never felt so right, so complete.

"Holy cow!" Marc exclaimed, tugging his hand away.

Melanie laughed at his childlike reaction, taking as much pleasure in his response as she had in her own. "Weird, isn't it?"

He gently put his hand back again. But this time, the tender emotion erupting inside Melanie was almost too much to bear.

If only things had been different....

"What's it like?" Marc quietly broke into her thoughts. "I want to know everything you're feeling."

Melanie told him.

Marc felt as if someone had completely pulled the earth out from under his feet as he watched myriad emotions cross Mel's face.

She finally broke eye contact. "I think he's tired himself out."

He took that as his cue to remove his hand, and he did, however reluctantly.

For a moment there, one sweet, miraculous moment, he'd felt connected to Mel in a way he never had before. Gone were the reasons they shouldn't be together. Gone were any doubts he or she might have had in the past. It had just been the two of them—and their baby.

He didn't want it to end.

She started to turn away. He gently caught her arm.

"I have something to show you, Melanie."

Her eyes widened slightly, most likely at his use of her full name.

Despite all the times he'd visualized this moment during the long drive from Manchester, he still fumbled with the damn velvet pouch as he slid it out of his back pocket. It fell to the ground between them.

Both of them stood staring at it, unmoving.

Then Marc knelt, staying there on the soft grass as he revealed the emerald ring blanketed in a pool of white silk.

He cleared his throat, forcing himself to look at her even though it appeared she didn't know quite what to do. "I love you, Mel. There's no way you can't know that. Baby or no baby, I want to marry you." Her hands covered her stomach. "But of course I'm glad there is a baby," he said quickly.

Her skin glowed a warm rose in the early afternoon sunshine as she whispered, "Tell me why I should believe you, Marc."

He swallowed hard. How did he go about doing that? "Would it help if I told you I bought the ring the day after you got shot? That I got this harebrained idea, after you asked me if I loved you, that what you really wanted was to get married?" He grimaced. "Only the idea turned out to be not so dumb, because the day I came over here to propose to you was the same day I found out you were engaged to Craig."

He cleared his throat and looked at the ring that had paled in comparison to the one she had been wearing two weeks earlier.

"It may have taken me a long time to realize it, but you were right back then, you know, when you asked if I loved you. I did love you. I do. Only I didn't know for sure until the day I nearly lost you in the chapel."

Mel stared at him long and hard, a suspicious dampness in her eyes. He wanted to groan but kept it in check. He supposed this was one of those times when women were allowed to cry. Even Mel. Especially Mel.

Then she turned away from him and moved toward the house.

"Mel!" He scrambled to his feet. "I'm serious. Look—"

He searched his pockets as he hurried after her. "I've even got the receipt to prove it."

As quickly as she turned away, she turned back, catapulting herself into his arms and nearly knocking him over. He stood stupidly, holding the ring in one hand, the receipt in the other, as she pressed her body against his, their baby very noticeably between them. He couldn't see her face, and she was squeezing him so hard he couldn't breathe.

"Mel, you're killing me here."

She threw her head back and laughed, then kissed him full on the mouth. "Why couldn't you have said all that three months ago, you big dope?"

He frowned. "What? You're killing me?"

Her smile softened. "Yeah. That, too."

He opened his mouth to respond, then refrained. "Does this mean what I think it means?"

Her eyes sparkled more brightly than the gem in his hand. "Yes, it may scare me to death, but it means exactly that."

Everything that had swirled around like pieces from different puzzles three months ago suddenly settled into place as he looked into her face. Never had he been so sure that he was doing the right thing.

He swept her into his arms and started marching toward the house, ignoring her laughing demands to be let down.

He grinned at her. "Uh-uh. Not until we're standing in front of a real pastor...."

Heart of the West

A brand-new Harlequin continuity series
begins in July 1999
with

Husband for Hire
by
Susan Wiggs

Beautician Twyla McCabe was Dear Abby
with a blow-dryer, listening to everyone else's
troubles. But now her well-meaning customers
have gone too far. No way was she attending
the Hell Creek High School Reunion with Rob
Carter, M.D. Who would believe a woman
who dyed hair for a living could be engaged
to such a hunk?

Here's a preview!

CHAPTER ONE

"THIS ISN'T FOR the masquerade. This is for me."

"What's for you?"

"This."

Rob didn't move fast, but with a straightforward deliberation she found oddly thrilling. He gripped Twyla by the upper arms and pulled her to him, covering her mouth with his.

Dear God, a kiss. She couldn't remember the last time a man had kissed her. And what a kiss. It was everything a kiss should be—sweet, flavored with strawberries and wine and driven by an underlying passion that she felt surging up through him, creating an answering need in her. She rested her hands on his shoulders and let her mouth soften, open. He felt wonderful beneath her hands, his muscles firm, his skin warm, his mouth... She just wanted to drown in him, drown in the passion. If he was faking his ardor, he was damned good. When he stopped kissing her, she stepped back. Her disbelieving fingers went to her mouth, lightly touching her moist, swollen lips.

"That...wasn't in the notes," she objected weakly.

"I like to ad–lib every once in a while."

"I need to sit down." Walking backward, never taking her eyes off him, she groped behind her and found the Adirondack-style porch swing. *Get a grip,* she told herself. *It was only a kiss.*

"I think," he said mildly, "it's time you told me just why you were so reluctant to come back here for the reunion."

"And why I had to bring a fake fiancé as a shield?"

Very casually, he draped his arm along the back of the porch swing. "I'm all ears, Twyla. Why'd I have to practically hog–tie you to get you back here?"

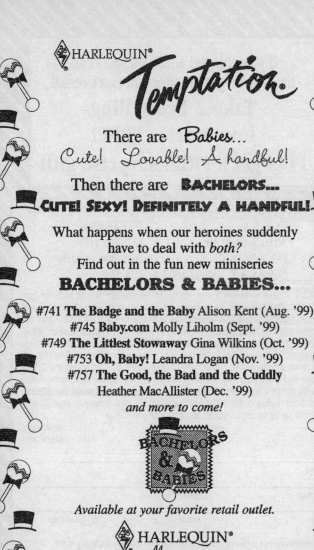

If you enjoyed what you just read,
then we've got an offer you can't resist!

Take 2 bestselling love stories FREE!

Plus get a FREE surprise gift!

HARLEQUIN®

Temptation

It's hot...and it's out of control!

BLAZE

This summer we're turning up the heat.
Look for this bold, provocative,
ultra-sexy book—by one of Temptation®'s
best-loved authors!

#744 PURE TEMPTATION
Vicki Lewis Thompson
August 1999

Summer Project: Lose virginity. At twenty-six,
Tess Blakely finds that her innocence is getting
embarassing. But growing up in a small town with four
big brothers was as effective as wearing a chastity belt.
Although she's read countless books on the subject,
it's past time for her to experience the *real* thing.
All she has to do is find a partner. And her best friend,
Jeremiah "Mac" MacDougal, is looking *very* good....

BLAZE—red-hot reads from
Temptation®!

Available at your favorite retail outlet.

HARLEQUIN®
Makes any time special ™

COMING NEXT MONTH

#741 THE BADGE AND THE BABY Alison Kent
Bachelors & Babies

Detective Joel Wolfsley was stuck with a baby! He adored his niece, but it was impossible to keep up with the munchkin while he was on crutches. Joel's delectable next-door neighbor came to the rescue. Willa Darling had a knack for mothering, even if her "babies" were of the canine variety.... She had a way with sexy uncles, too.

#742 WHO'S THE BOSS? Jill Shalvis

Poor little rich girl Caitlin Taylor was in dire straits when her father died, leaving her nothing but an office job and a stack of bills. Her new boss was a computer whiz with an attitude, and no happier than Caitlin with the arrangement. If Joe hadn't worshiped Caitlin's father, he would have fired Calamity Jane on day one. But he let her stay, and soon he never wanted to let her go....

#743 THE ROCKY RIDGE MAN Meredith March

Advertising exec Sonya Duncan had no use for cowboys, except as a filler for a pair of Rocky Ridge blue jeans. Just her luck that the only man whose gorgeous rear fit the bill happened to be the genuine article. Clint Silver was no more cooperative than a steer being branded, and Sonya had to use all her womanly wiles to corral the sexy rancher.

#744 PURE TEMPTATION Vicki Lewis Thompson
Blaze

Summer Project: Lose virginity. At twenty-six, Tess Blakely's innocence was embarrassing. But growing up in a small town with four big brothers...well, she might as well have worn a chastity belt. She'd read all about sex—now she just needed to experience it with the right man. Her best friend, Jeremiah "Mac" MacDougal, was looking very tempting....